THE ZIGGURAT

Chris Nicholls

THE ZIGGURAT

THE BODLEY HEAD
London

For Dasha

First published in 1991 by
The Bodley Head Children's Books
an imprint of The Random Century Group Ltd
20 Vauxhall Bridge Road, London SW1V 2SA

Random Century Australia Pty Ltd
20 Alfred Street, Sydney, NSW 2061

Random Century New Zealand Ltd
PO Box 40–086, Glenfield, Auckland 10, New Zealand

Random Century South Africa Pty Ltd
PO Box 337, Bergvlei 2012, South Africa

Photoset by Speedset Ltd, Ellesmere Port

Printed and bound in Great Britain by
Mackays of Chatham, PLC

British Library Cataloguing in Publication Data
is available

ISBN 0–370–31487–5

Robyn : Explanation

We were all three sitting on a slab of rock just inside one of the Pikestone caves. Well, Laura and Jake were sitting but I was kneeling, gazing out of an opening – a sort of window – in the side of the cave, across the sunlit valley to the hill the other side, on which stands the Ziggurat. You can't actually see the Ziggurat from the cave because it's well over the top of the hill and much higher up, but it's there all right.

Then a half-thought which had been jigging around in my mind for months suddenly became a whole thought, and I looked down towards Laura and Jake and announced that I was going to write the complete story of what happened with Steve Mallinson.

'You'll never do it,' said Jake. 'It'd take far too long.'

'People do write books,' I retorted.

'Yeah, I read one once,' said Jake. 'And it wasn't written by someone just starting on their GCSE year either. Anyway, all that stuff happened so long ago. Who cares now?'

'I've got the summer holidays. And *I* care. I want to show exactly how it was, so that people will know how to stop it ever happening again.'

'The only trouble is,' Laura said thoughtfully, 'that you'd have to write about me and Jake as well as yourself. And I don't think you understand us well enough.'

1

I was offended by that, of course. 'OK, then,' I said. 'Write your own versions if you don't think you're going to like mine.'

'I've got a better idea,' said Laura.

The book you have follows Laura's idea. And I'm not so certain that it shows exactly what I wanted it to show any more . . .

Robyn: First Encounter with Steve Mallinson

I remember that every time I thought about going back to school again I got like this hard fist in my stomach, clutching at my insides, squeezing them into a tight ball. It was fine out at Pikestone during holidays, miles away from it, but it was a different world at school. Steve Mallinson's world, mainly.

It wouldn't have been so bad if the first half of the term hadn't ended the way it had. I wasn't sorry, because I hadn't done the wrong thing, but I was scared. You just didn't cross Steve, and I knew that if it hadn't been the day before the holiday began, something would have happened to me then. And now all I knew was that something *would* happen to me, because everyone said that Steve never forgot.

I can see him even now, with his film-star face, giving me that dark thoughtful look, with a pair of his thugs hovering near as if they were itching to get on with doing something vile. And around us the dirty wooden walls of what he and everyone else called his 'office' – a deserted bit in the school grounds completely surrounded by disused mobile classrooms. There was no chance of any teacher coming in there because they never did. In any case Steve was too careful to get caught actually hurting someone.

'Well, Robyn,' he said, all calm and threatening, 'so you don't like the way we run things, eh?' Steve always

3

said 'we', not 'I'. Then he went on before I had time even to breathe, 'That's a funny name for a girl, isn't it? Robyn.'

'It's Australian,' I managed to get out.

'Australian, eh? Down under, eh? You come from there, then?'

'My mum did.'

'Mm. Australia. They don't do a lot of biking there, do they?'

'I don't know, I've never –'

'Too far to bike anywhere, I should think. Wide open spaces.'

He seemed to be going all dreamy trying to imagine Australia, then he suddenly turned on me sharply.

'So that's why you mightn't wanna buy bike insurance. Well, I could understand that – it's your risk. But don't forget that a lot of kids that've taken that risk have been sorry – even some that don't use bikes.'

There was a snort of a laugh from one of the thugs beside him – Martin Dwyer, the fish-eyed, pale, slimy one that everyone reckoned did the damage to the bikes.

'So as I say,' Steve went on, 'that's your risk. What I object to – what I really do *not* like – is you meddling in what's none of your business. Trying to persuade other kids not to join in the schemes. That is not fair of you.'

I just managed to hold myself from saying something like, 'It's you that's not fair,' because I guessed he was trying to make me angry so he'd have an excuse to get angry back. He just loved playing with his victims like that.

'Well, if you think you don't need bike insurance – and you will – you might be forgetting what's included in it. I mean, have you ever thought how sad it'd be if your homework always got torn up before you had a chance to hand it in?'

I shook my head.

'No? Think about it, then. Or there's just plain getting hurt. That's covered in the bike insurance too, you know. For some people that's a hell of a risk to take.'

He stared hard at me for a long time till I felt I was a fly he was just about to swat, then said, 'I'll give you this holiday to think it all over. But think hard, mind. Think really carefully.'

He waved me off out of his office, but as I was going he made one last point.

'Oh, and don't bother mentioning this conversation to anyone else, will you, or you're going to need some very heavy insurance indeed.'

There was no need for him to spell out what he meant – what might happen if I did talk. They had it all sewn up, for one simple reason: as well as the thugs he always had with him, Steve knew people outside the school who'd do whatever he wanted. Two of them had been slung out nearly a year back for assaulting a teacher, and now they had nothing better to do than hang around making trouble. But everyone said there were others too, even worse – real criminal types.

Just twice in the time I'd been at the school, he'd used these 'friends' of his. When I first arrived, I heard that someone in the third year had been off for three weeks with injuries – I never found out what exactly, and I hadn't really believed it.

The second time, though, was someone in our year, Little Darren Williams, who wouldn't hurt a fly, had limped into school with his left eye so black and swollen that he couldn't see with it. My friend Laura told me

5

Darren had been walking home when two big lads had overtaken him, one each side. As they went past, one of them had shoved his elbow back into Darren's face and the other had kicked back with his heel right on to Darren's kneecap and down his shin. It was dark and he never saw their faces, but he was sure they weren't from school.

At first he told his parents he'd fallen over, but they got something like the truth out of him in the end. Except that he hadn't dared tell them the main truth – about Steve – not even when they got the police in.

And Laura said the only reason Steve had done that to him was because Darren had seen him showing off in front of some girls, trying to do wheelies on his racer, and then he'd slipped on a patch of ice and fallen off. The girls had giggled, and so little Darren, who was just passing, had laughed too. Steve got him by the lapels of his coat and practically spat in his face, going, 'You don't laugh at *me*!' Darren said Steve looked almost crazy, he was so furious – eyes bulging, purple in the face, quivering like a loony.

So that was why, when I went shakily back to the main playground and my friends all came crowding round me wanting to know what he'd said, I didn't tell them much.

I did tell Laura, though, partly because she is my best friend and partly because I needed to tell someone, but mainly because we live near each other in Pikestone village, just on the edge of the Pikestone estate. That isn't a housing estate, by the way, but an estate in the old sense of the word – it's all land that used to belong to one big house (only it's not a house now but a ruin) and it's right out in the country, about five miles from town.

So Laura's almost the only person I do see from school at weekends and half terms and holidays.

Sometimes I wonder if we'd be best friends if we weren't thrown together like that, because she is odd. I like her a lot when we go exploring in Pikestone and she makes up these weird stories about all the different places in it. On the other hand she too often mixes fact with fiction so that even she doesn't seem to know which is which. I guess you could call her an entertaining liar a lot of the time.

That was why it probably wasn't wise telling Laura about my interview with Steve. But as I said, I had to tell someone. Oh, I tried telling Mum, of course, but Mum was expecting a baby soon so I didn't want to make it sound too frightening. As a result all she said was, 'Well, I should just keep out of their way for a bit.' Then she added, 'You won't worry your dad about it, will you?'

Even if she hadn't said that, I wouldn't have tried telling him. I don't think I could ever have got him to believe it was as serious as I knew it was. He works in this cosy little craft pottery business down in the village, where everything's gentle and organized, and if you ever try to tell him what a jungle it is out there, he shuts off.

Laura said two things when the holiday was coming to an end and my worries finally burst out of me. The first meant exactly what I'd expected her to say, but the way she put it seemed a bit odd to me.

'I don't know why you bother with him, Robyn.'

'What do you mean, me bother with him? It was him bothering me.'

'Yes, but you started it, trying to get people to make a fuss about the usual payments.'

'Just because I don't fancy paying him thirty pence a half term for a bit of rubbish and then another fifty to protect myself from him and his mates, is that *me* making a fuss?'

'Well, the extra fifty's your own fault for trying to start trouble. Everyone else just pays up thirty and they aren't bothered again.'

'Then it's about time they stopped. I mean, it's about time *we* stopped.'

'Go ahead and try stopping. But don't expect me to feel sorry for you when he catches up with you.'

The second thing, which she followed with at once, may sound even odder to you, though I was quite used to it by then.

'Anyway,' she went on, 'he's got the power, you know.'

'I know he's got the power!' I snapped back. She didn't have to tell me that. I'd seen it. I'd felt it close to.

'No, I mean you can't win against him. You haven't got the power.'

'What do you mean?' I said, irritated as hell. 'That's what it's all about. We've got to organize people against him.'

'It wouldn't do any good.' She spoke in a dreamy sort of way, then added, 'Because of magic' – as if that explained it.

'Oh, magic!' I said disgustedly. Of course I knew Laura had this thing about magic, but it was a bit too much to take now, with the reality of Steve to face looming closer and closer. 'Oh yeah, let's go and find a book of spells and change Steve Mallinson into the toad he really is.'

'Magic is real, you know.' She was still dreamy, not

responding to my sarcasm at all. 'It can be used. He uses it.'

Then she suddenly snapped out of her dreaminess and said, 'We'll have to talk it over in the Ziggurat.'

But it was too late to go up to the Ziggurat then, so we arranged to meet up there the next day, the last day of the half-term holiday. I thought about what Laura had said. Don't imagine she's one of those kids that never seem to grow up and still go on believing in witches and fairies and suchlike. Whatever she meant by 'magic', I knew it wasn't anything like that, but I wished I had a better idea what she did mean.

Jake : Going Up

It was turning out to be a dangerous climb, and I knew I shouldn't be doing it alone. The cliff hadn't looked sheer when I'd first started up it – more like a steep slope – but it had got steeper and steeper, and now it was very nearly straight up. And although the drop beneath me wasn't quite a direct fall all the way – I wasn't going to be so stupid as to look down and see *how* direct – there'd be absolutely no chance of stopping myself if I did slip. I could surely break a leg, at least. And who'd hear me shouting for help then, in this wilderness?

In fact it was all very stupid of me, and if it hadn't been for catching sight from down below of that strange turret poking out of the trees somewhere up there, I'd never have dreamed of trying the cliff at all.

Finding a bit of a ledge for both feet, and with one firm handhold anyway, I did risk looking up. It was hard to tell exactly, against the bright sky, but there didn't really seem to be so much further to go – perhaps another couple of metres – a good deal better than trying to get back down now. I pushed aside the question of how I was going to get down once I'd finally made it to the top. There'd just have to be another way.

It wouldn't have been so bad if it was only the brambles sprouting and trailing here and there over the cliff face. They made things difficult, but they weren't dangerous the way this crumbling red sandstone was. You saw a firm-looking handhold above you but you never knew if it was actually going to be firm or come off in your hand the moment you put any pressure on it. The only good thing about it was that its being softer in some places than others had allowed the weather to scoop out hundreds of holes and cracks and ledges all over the place. And its surface was good and rough for my trainers, not slippery.

My hand and feet were aching with holding the same position for too long. It was time to move – and actually it didn't look so difficult now. There was a long crack almost in reach that ran slantwise right up to the top. Once I'd got my toes into that I'd be able to shuffle sideways all the way up it.

A shallow toehold, then both hands in the crack, left hand up a bit further to a sticking-out knob of worn stone, and I was on my way. There was just one more nasty moment when I got a bit too sure of myself, feeling my feet secure, reaching round for anything to help me on – I grasped at what I thought was a little moss-covered ledge, only to find it was practically nothing else but moss, with a little soil underneath. It crumbled away as soon as I touched it. Even while I was clawing at the stone beneath it to get my balance back, I could hear the bits of it pattering down into the bushes below me.

But a few seconds later I was bending my body over the top, levering myself forward on my hands, legs dragged up behind till my knees were over too. Then I rolled over to sit on the edge, legs dangling over space, looking out and down to where I'd climbed from. I'd made it.

Now I could see it from up here, the layout of this

part of the estate seemed pretty simple. A straight, narrow valley – so narrow and steep-sided at times that it was more like a gorge – ran the whole length of the estate, maybe further. I was at the top of one side of the valley, looking across to the much barer top of the other side. I hadn't explored that part at all yet, but on the other hand that was the part my dad said was more under control, so it was less interesting and anyway, over there I might bump into him any moment.

So much for seeing the layout from above. When you were actually down in those bushes and giant ferns and trees below, trying to steer yourself away from the outbreaks of bramble thickets and massed nettles, it seemed a lot less simple.

More than ever I missed having my gang with me. Pikestone would have been the most fantastic place to play in, and all those difficulties and dangers would just have been extra adventures.

Behind me, there was only a short stretch of bare rock and bits of wiry grass before the bushes and tall trees began again, just like down below. Being an estate warden's son, I could recognize rhododendron bushes when I saw them; I also knew that although they could spread without help, they didn't start up on their own – they had to be planted. Up here too, then, must have been part of the estate's massive gardens at one time.

I was far too close to the bushes to be able to see over them to the turret thing I was chasing, and now I had only the vaguest idea which direction it would lie in, so I gave up that project for today. I might come across it by chance anyway, because I'd have to push on forward if I wanted to be back home in time to help Dad get tea, and not being able to face going down the way I'd come up meant that I'd got to try and get round to the end of the valley – well, the end of the steep-sided bit anyway. So I chose the part where the rhododendrons looked thinnest and went in.

The good thing about rhododendrons is that they stop nettles and stuff from growing underneath them, so they form passages and tunnels and sort of caves. You get blocked by low branches sometimes and have to crawl, but it's quite exciting – like jungle without any nasties.

So I went on, able to stand up occasionally, but mostly stooping and pushing branches aside, trying to steer myself in a straightish line, till suddenly the bushes thinned out, there was long grass, and then I was out on a path. It ran straight across the direction I'd been going in, and it looked used, but not too used, almost grown over by brambles in parts and quite muddy in places.

Either way it seemed to be curving gradually round between the bushes, away from the direction I really wanted to go in, which was back. On the other hand, wherever it led to, it would get me to somewhere a lot quicker than climbing or pushing through undergrowth. It might even take me past that turret or whatever it was. I tossed a coin in my mind – heads right, tails left. The word 'tails' was the one that came to me first, so I chose left.

The path went on curving and curving till I felt sure it must have done nearly a full circle, and I was going to wind up back where I'd joined it – not that I'd have recognized the place if I had. It all looked the same – grass and bracken then bushes each side, trees above. In the muddy bits there were some footprints, mostly big but one or two smaller than mine. They were probably oldish footprints, I guessed.

But at last it changed. The path began to straighten out more and more, till I could see quite a way ahead, to where things seemed to be opening out into a clearing. Finally the bushes each side fell right away, the path gave one last twist, and there, a hundred metres or so in front of me at the far end of a large clearing, was this amazing tower.

When I say it was a tower, I don't mean one of those square, solid towers like there are on castles or churches. This one is round and quite narrow and tall, fantastically tall. Even at that distance I had to bend my head back to see the top of it – certainly the top I'd seen from below – and not one of the trees in the clearing came up to more than half its height. There aren't any other buildings anywhere around – just this great high stone thing standing alone, with the path leading to a dark opening at the bottom.

When you get to know it a bit, you often find yourself wondering *Why?* about it. Or *Who?* – who in the world could have spent all that time and trouble building this huge thing with no use you can begin to see, so far from anywhere? Was it maybe once part of a house or something, and the rest had fallen down? Or had it been meant as a sort of Nelson's column with a statue of some big hero on top, but the statue had never been made, or had fallen off or been nicked?

But that first time all I could think was just, *What on earth?* What was it? Was it hollow? Might there be people in it – or near it? And most important of all, What am I going to do about it?

Even though it was really getting pretty late, there was only one answer to that last question: I was going to have a much closer look at it. It just was not one of those things you can say, 'I'll come back and have a good look

14

at it tomorrow' about. It needed checking out *now*.

So I went on towards it, trying hard to be much quieter, just in case, keeping a careful eye out for signs of anyone around, and at the same time craning my head back further and further to see what could possibly be at the top of the thing.

It actually ends in a turret, a bit like on a lighthouse, with a little pointed roof, and round the bottom of the turret a square sort of platform. But there's one thing that hits you about that platform, almost before you notice anything else. There's a corner missing – just kind of torn off. Even though I hadn't yet begun to wonder *how* that bit fell out, it already seemed to be shouting *Danger!* at me. If you're ever looking up at a tall building, and the clouds behind it are moving away from you, it seems as if the building's falling towards you – and that was how it was when I stopped for a minute to stare up.

You can imagine that by the time I got right close to the opening in the base I was quite jumpy already, and the sight of steps inside, curling up and round out of sight, didn't help at all. They meant I'd got to try them: there just wasn't anywhere else to go, if you see what I mean – leastways, not for someone who was used to leading his gang everywhere and into everything we could get into.

I also knew that it was no good hesitating in front of these things. You had to go for it. So I pretended I had Sime and Lee and Mark behind me, going, 'Cor!' and 'Phew!' and 'What's it like up there?' The entrance and the steps were thick with dust, twigs, dead leaves, and they didn't look as if they'd been used for centuries, but I went straight in and started up them.

It's that first bit that's the second-worst part of going

15

up inside – the other is when you get to the top. It's bad because after the stairs have done perhaps one and a half turns, the light coming in from the entrance fades out, and suddenly you're in pitch-blackness. What's even worse, if you don't know, is the possibility that the thing might be falling to bits inside – some of those earlier steps look cracked and rotten enough. In other words, you might easily step out on to a step that wasn't there, and . . .

It was that thought that did for me. Even though I was feeling my way forward with my foot (I didn't like to use my hands in case I put them on – well, *something*) the idea of my foot meeting nothing at all just grew more and more scaring. I simply couldn't face going on and on and up like that. I went slower and slower. Then I came to a stop. And when I did that, the cold smell of the stone, and the dead silence, began to get to me. I turned round and started down again.

I hadn't done more than two or three steps down when I heard something that froze me where I was. *Footsteps, coming up, towards me.*

At first I could do nothing, I was so fixed with terror. I stood there, cold, breath heaving, hair rising on the back of my head. Then the footsteps hesitated, then stopped. Anything – *any*thing – would be better than meeting whoever it was in this total darkness, so I called out the first thing I could think of – 'Hello'. I say 'called out', but what actually did come out was a kind of dry squeak which didn't improve much when I tried a second time. 'Hello!'

There was a little pause before a doubtful-sounding voice – a woman's – came echoing up. 'I know you're up there robbing.'

I was still shaking like jelly, but at least I thought I

knew what the danger was now. I was just in ordinary plain trouble again, being accused of something I wasn't doing.

'No, I'm not,' I shouted down – my annoyance made it a bit less of a squeak. 'I was only having a look.'

This was met by silence, then more footsteps. I was not going to be caught in the dark by whoever it was, so I started to hurry down to meet them.

It was a fantastic relief when the light began to come back again, but it was also a worry because there was no sign of the other person at all, not right the way down, not even in the entrance. The word 'ghost' came into my mind, as I jumped the last three steps and bolted through the doorway, out into the open daylight.

But it wasn't a ghost. As my eyes slowly got used to the bright sunlight again, I began to see someone quite solid facing me, a girl perhaps near my age. In fact she was very solid, filling her jeans and check blouse almost to bursting, though you couldn't exactly call her fat. The only slightly unreal thing about her was the way the sun caught her frizzled fairish hair, surrounding her large face with light.

I realized in a flash how stupid I'd been to panic – those later footsteps had been going away from me, not coming on upwards!

'Hello,' said the girl. 'I'm Laura. Who are you?'

Laura: Three Stories

I could sense at once how terrified he was – or at any rate had been. He had quite a nice brown face, but at the moment it was pale, and his dark eyes were wild and panicky. He settled down a bit when I spoke, though, because I put a special calm into my voice for him.

'Jake,' he answered. 'God, you scared me. What did you want to say I was robbing the place for? There isn't anything up there to rob, is there?'

I saw what had happened at once. It made me laugh, and this was wrong, because he thought I was laughing at his fear. Boys don't like that.

'What's the big joke?' he said angrily. 'I suppose you think it's funny, creeping up on people and telling them they're thieves.'

And that only made me giggle even worse, so it was a while – and he just stood there scowling at me – before I could explain.

'Not "robbing"; "Robyn" – my friend, Robyn. What I said was, "I know you're up there, Robyn," because I thought you must be her playing a trick on me. We arranged to meet here at the Ziggurat, see, and I thought she'd got here first and gone on up.'

He went on scowling. 'What d'you mean, "she"? You said "Robin".'

'That's her name. Only it ends "Y-N" – it's Australian.'

18

He shook his head impatiently, as if Australia was too much to cope with at the moment, then asked, 'Well what's the Ziggurap, then, or whatever you said?'

I pointed behind him, and he looked round and nodded.

'Why's it called the Ziggurap?'

'Because it is,' I said. 'Why are you called Jake?'

'Jake's a name,' he said. 'Other kids have it. Sometimes it's short for Jacob, sometimes it isn't. Mine isn't. There. Now tell me what "Ziggurap" means.'

'It's "rat", not "rap", and it means a sort of tower.'

'Big surprise,' he said sarcastically. He was still frightened and angry, and I could see that I was going to have to tell him a story to quieten him down. I chose quickly from my stock – but carefully, because it had to be believable as well as making him feel tough and strong again.

'It's a Roman ziggurat,' I began. 'When the Roman armies came to Britain they built towers like this all over the country, so they could control the English people from them. They could go to the top and see for miles what everyone was doing, and if anyone was getting an army together to attack them. Most of the other towers have fallen down, but this one hasn't yet. You see that platform up at the top?'

He turned and looked up, so I knew my story was working.

'Well, a Roman guard used to have to walk round and round that platform all the time, and that was why they made it so narrow and didn't put any fence or anything round it – so that the guard wouldn't dare go into a daydream or go to sleep on his feet. He just had to keep watching and watching.'

19

'Or he'd fall off, you mean. Wow! But what about that bit out of it? How did that happen?'

I suddenly decided not to give him my Roman answer to that because there was too much about fear in it, and that was the last thing he needed just now. I chose one of Robyn's favourites instead.

'That was years later – hundreds of years later. Two men were quarrelling over a lady they both loved, and one of them chased the other to the top, but, you see, when the Romans built the ziggurats they made the platforms only strong enough to hold one person – on purpose. They didn't want two guards being up there chatting away and not keeping a lookout.'

'Yeah' – he was getting quite excited about it now – 'and I suppose it made it safer because if an enemy did manage to creep up, they wouldn't dare go out and attack the Roman guard, because if they did they'd both get killed.'

'Maybe. Anyway, these two men went up there, and the one whose wife the lady was went out first, and he tried to warn the other one that wanted her that he wasn't to come out. But the other one thought it was just a trick to stop him, so he went on out –'

'– and the platform broke under him. Served him right.'

'No, that isn't what happened. The husband kept shouting to him to stop, but he wouldn't, and the moment he put his weight on to the platform it broke under the husband and it was him that fell to his death.'

'Yow, tough! So I suppose the one that didn't die married the lady.'

'No, she wouldn't have anything to do with him after he'd killed her husband. She just shut herself away in her house till the day she died. She said she'd lost the most beautiful thing in her life, so she'd spend the rest of it collecting beautiful things, and she gradually filled her house with paintings and carpets and china and ornaments.'

'Mm.' This was the part of the story that Robyn loved best, but his eyes were beginning to wander. He was losing interest.

'Where do you live?' he asked.

So we began to swap information, starting off with the basic, boring facts. Jake was nearly twelve; so was I. Jake had only just arrived in the area, as I knew; I'd lived here all my life. Jake's father was the new warden for the Pikestone estate; my parents kept the Pikestone village post office. Jake was obviously lonely, because he seemed glad to know that Robyn and me lived down in the village, just near, but he looked disappointed when I told him there weren't any boys of his own age there.

'Are you used to having lots of friends around?' I asked.

'Not half!' he said. 'Where I was before, there was a whole gang of us, but you see –'

He stopped for a second and gave me a sort of sideways look. Then suddenly he was talking quite differently, telling me his story. It was a sad one, although Jake said it all in such a very matter-of-fact way that it was almost as if the story was about someone else, not himself.

He was an only child, and his mother had died a little under a year ago. His father had tried to keep going, but in the end he'd found it impossible to stay living and working in the same place where everything reminded him of his wife, and he'd decided he'd have to get a new job in a completely different part of the country. He knew this wasn't right for Jake, who wanted more than anything to stay where he was – where everything was familiar – and especially to stay in the new big school he'd just moved up to with all his friends.

At first Jake had asked why his father couldn't move away alone, leaving him where he was. The mum of one of his friends had said she'd look after Jake during the term, and he could visit his dad in the holidays, and even sometimes at weekends, because it was less than a hundred miles away. And in fact they'd arranged all that.

Then one day Jake went to find his dad out on the estate where he worked, to give him a message. And he saw his dad before his dad saw him. He was sitting on a tree-stump, crying. Instead of giving the message, Jake ran all the way back to his house and telephoned his friend's mum to say he wasn't staying after all. He was going away with his dad.

Naturally his dad was furious at first, because he didn't know what had made Jake change his mind like that, but eventually he agreed, and Jake knew he was glad. They'd moved here only two days ago.

'Are you sorry you did that?' I asked.

'Of course I am, in a way. But what else could I do? I mean, it's nice here, and I like exploring it all, but most of the time I just wish I was back home. And I'm not looking forward to starting school tomorrow, I can tell you. Coming in in the middle of the summer term, and where I don't know a single person.'

'You know me.'

'Yeah, but . . .'

He wanted to say that I was only a girl, but he was too polite. I started to tell him a bit about the school, then he suddenly looked down at his watch.

'Wow, I'm late! Dad'll kill me. It'll take me ages to get back too.'

'If your dad's the new warden, I suppose you're living in Pikestone Lodge.'

'Yeah, and I've got that cliff to get down somehow, unless – you don't know a quicker way, do you?'

'You came straight up the side of the valley!' I knew those climbs, and wouldn't have dared to do any of them myself.

'Yes, and it was murder. I don't think –'

'Take that path there, out of the clearing, then when it forks, go right, down the hill, and it takes you straight by the lodge, with no cliffs or anything, and I'll see you on the bus tomorrow. Right?'

'Ta,' he said, and he actually gave me a nice smile to go with it. He took a few steps down the path I'd shown him, then suddenly stopped and turned, pointed up at the top of the Ziggurat.

'I tell you what,' he said. 'It's really scary up there, isn't it? Specially when you get round the far side of that platform.'

I knew he was lying, but I also knew he felt he had to. I nodded as if I believed him. He gave me a wave and ran off, leaving me to continue waiting for Robyn.

While I waited I thought a lot about Jake. There was something you couldn't trust about him and something you could, but I didn't know which was which, and that's unusual for me.

Robyn was late again, as she always was. She could never understand why I insisted on us meeting up here instead of walking up from the village together, so I suppose that hanging around waiting for her was the price I had to pay for having my own way.

But there's an awful lot of things Robyn doesn't

23

understand, because she's too down-to-earth. She likes the Ziggurat, but doesn't understand why it's important. She only partly understands the point of my stories. Most of all, she doesn't understand why she can't fight Steve Mallinson – not yet, anyway. She has absolutely no magic at all in her.

Jake : Starting Off

That first day at Ashleigh High was about as bad as I'd
been afraid it might be. No worse, but as bad. I suppose
those things almost always are, but don't forget I was
arriving in the middle of a term, and I was the only
person new in a place I hadn't even seen before.

I'd also been right to think it wouldn't make any
difference that I knew Laura. She gets on the bus the
stop before I do, and of course she'd got a friend next to
her. She smiled and said, 'Hi,' but turned back to her
friend at once, and there didn't seem any point in even
sitting near her.

Even when we got there she wasn't much help. We
piled off the bus opposite the school gates, went across
and through, and there we were, somewhere in the
middle of this huge collection of assorted buildings. I
did have the nerve then to run after Laura and ask
where she thought I ought to go first. But all she did was
giggle to her friend a bit embarrassed, and say, 'I
dunno, really.' It was her friend who said, 'Oh, he'll
have to go to the secretary and ask there, won't he?' and
then even, 'Come on. Let's show him the way.'

So they led me through this jostling maze of yards
and alleyways outside, then corridors inside. On the
way Laura's friend introduced herself as Robyn (which
I'd guessed already from Laura's mentioning her the
day before) and said I'd be almost bound to be in the

same year group as them, but maybe not in the same tutor group.

Back in my old school we just had 'forms', so of course I hadn't a clue what a year group or a tutor group were. I was just about to ask, when we were brought to a stop by a couple of big, older lads standing in front of us, blocking our way. One of them looked almost like an adult, with a stubbly face and short-cropped sandy hair; he was short, but built as solid as a weightlifter. The other was quite different – pale, thin and thin-faced and with these really cold eyes. If the first looked as if he'd hurt you without thinking about it, the second looked as if he'd enjoy it.

I thought at first it might be me they wanted to know about, being new, but they weren't interested in me – only Robyn.

The short one spoke to her almost as though he'd had to learn his message by heart to be sure of getting it right.

'Steve wants a word with you at breaktime.'

'Yeah,' said the thin one, with a nasty grin. 'He wants to know if you've been doing any good thinking recently. Know what I mean?'

Robyn just stood there, bowing her head, nodding.

'In the office,' said the short one.

'Don't be late,' added the other in a mocking sort of way, as though he knew she wouldn't dare.

Then they stood aside to let us go on. Robyn started whispering urgently to Laura; but tagging along behind, I couldn't at all catch what they were saying, except for one of Laura's answers.

'Just exactly what we decided, Robyn.' I heard it because she was speaking fiercely, as if it really mattered. 'You can*not* win.'

26

I wouldn't have asked what was going on even if there'd been time, because it wasn't any of my business, but in any case next minute we'd arrived in a sort of foyer place where Robyn pointed at a big glass window with a woman sitting at a desk behind it.

'That's the secretary,' she said, pointing. 'She'll tell you what to do.'

Her voice sounded weak and trembly, and her little face was quite a few shades paler. Then they both turned and went off back the way we'd come, leaving me to get on with the unpleasant business of starting school.

I won't bore you too much with all that – that feeling of total confusion, the embarrassment of trying to know what you should be doing and getting it wrong, and generally looking like a complete dope . . .

Just one example. After having to hang about till the whole school had quietened down, I was eventually taken along to meet my group tutor, who was called Mrs Carmel – the secretary kindly wrote it down on a slip of paper for me, so that I wouldn't forget it. The only trouble was that her writing wasn't too clear, so that when I was suddenly led into this classroom and just left there to make my own way to the front, with everyone staring at me, I went forward and asked, 'Excuse me, miss. Are you' – looking at my slip of paper – 'Mrs Camel?'

Of course everyone fell about for ages, and she got ratty as hell – not with me, though she wasn't too pleased with me either. Later I learned that all the kids always called her 'the Camel' behind her back, and she hated it.

Something in me decided then and there that I was

not going to let myself spend a lot of time in that school being a joke waiting for people to laugh at. I was going to be one of those that led the laughing, just as soon as I could get a few mates together.

Not that there was much promise in my first contact. Mrs Carmel appointed a nice but dozy lad called Dave Abbot to 'look after' me. It turned out that Dave was mad on scuba diving and almost nothing else, whereas I knew so little about it myself that I'd always vaguely thought that scuba were a kind of fish, like tuna. So our conversation pretty quickly came to a full stop, even before the first break, and I left him then, saying I could look after myself.

I'd already worked out that the thing to do during the break was what I was best at and could only really do alone – exploring; getting to know the layout of the place. It wasn't difficult to pretend that all the other kids milling around were like patches of nettles or brambles or rhododendron bushes, to be skirted round and between. Or like wasps and bees – they only sting you if you interfere with them.

Nosing around, getting further away from the gangs and the pairs and the giggling groups, I came to a part of the school grounds where there were some temporary-looking buildings which didn't appear much used, and I was just passing the end of a passageway between two of these, when down the far end I saw Robyn. Even with her back to me, there was no mistaking that thin figure and dark bob of hair. And she was standing on one leg, rubbing the other behind it nervously, like I'd noticed she was when she'd met those two toughs earlier on.

It was the meeting she'd been told about, of course! I'd completely forgotten, what with my own problems.

Steve. That must be him in front of that same pair, leaning over Robyn, right up close, the way a teacher does to tell you off about something.

For a minute I half thought of going along to see if she was all right. It looked like a plain case of some kind of bullying to me, and I could maybe use my being new to some advantage – you know, just pretend I was lost, simply as a way of disturbing them, breaking things up a bit. The Head at my last school had worked very hard on trying to stamp out bullying and he'd pretty well succeeded too. So bullying was just an idea to me, not something I was used to seeing actually happen, and I didn't know how to handle it at all.

In the end my more careful side got the better of me. What was going on wasn't any of my business. It looked very private, whatever it was, and no one was actually hurting or even touching Robyn – I saw her take a tiny step back from Steve, but there didn't seem to be any good reason for it, and he didn't follow it up. Anyway, she might not want me to interfere. I knew absolutely nothing about anything. I could wind up in trouble myself without having helped her in the slightest, or I could even make things worse for her.

So when one of the lads caught sight of me and yelled out, 'Oi! Come 'ere, you,' I just did a swift disappearing trick, leaving them to it, and came away feeling a bit bad about it. It wasn't till some time later that I learned what had been going on, and I was glad to find then that I'd been right. There really wasn't much I could have done.

Robyn : Steve
Mallinson Rules

I think my real problem is that I've had it drilled into me by both Mum and Dad ever since I was in my pram that it's wrong to tell lies. Otherwise I could simply have told Steve, 'Yes, sir. No, sir. I'll do whatever you want, sir,' and carried on working against him behind his back – only with a bit more care and cunning than I'd shown before.

The trouble was, I just didn't seem able to do that. I'm one of those kids that if a teacher says, 'Stand up those who were talking', I'm on my feet almost after the first two words. In fact, I have a job not to stand up even if I *wasn't* talking!

So when I met Steve (backed as usual by Martin Dwyer and Gary Talbot) and the first thing he asked was, 'Well, have you been doing some good hard thinking, then?' the little speech Laura and I had worked out for me to say blew out of my mind like dust.

Instead, I came out with a very trembly, 'Yes, but I still don't agree with you.'

I mean, just imagine – saying that kind of thing to Steve and his mates, of all people. And not even saying it strongly, as if I meant it.

I suppose the most that can be said for it is that it did produce a response. Steve stared at me, just blinking several times, as if he didn't understand what I'd said. Then his eyes began to bulge as though he was going to be furious, but he quickly got a grip on himself and turned to look round at his thugs, giving a sneery little laugh that was nearer a spit. They did much the same (but then they always did what Steve did).

'So you don't agree with me,' he said, calm now, moving a step closer. 'And what's that supposed to mean to me?'

It was my turn not to know how to answer. 'I just – I just – I just don't think you . . .' I tailed off, having given Steve the perfect cue.

'Too bloody right, you don't think you. But people who don't think have to be taught, right?'

I nodded. He was beginning to enjoy himself now – play-acting the patient teacher with a stupid kid, but with a real menace behind his act.

'That's what we come to school to learn, isn't it? How to think. And little children that won't learn have to be taught a *sharp* lesson.'

He said the word 'sharp' with such force that it seemed he was almost going to accompany it with an actual slap or something, and I flinched just a bit. But at the same instant Gary Talbot suddenly shouted out, 'Oi! Come 'ere, you,' at someone behind me – someone I suppose he must have seen looking into the office – and Steve controlled himself.

And that, I knew already, was one of the main reasons for his success. He was actually very careful in spite of the huge difficulty he had bottling up his violent temper. He almost never got into direct trouble himself. Other people did his dirty work for him, especially those people he knew outside school.

Seeing him control himself like that made me suddenly realize I had nothing to fear – nothing immediate, that is. A speck of my courage began to

31

come back – enough for me to get my wits together to say what was probably the most cowardly thing I've ever said in my life!

'I'll do my best not to trouble you again.'

It was part of the speech Laura had made me rehearse with her. I hated myself even as I said it. I felt as though I was betraying some actual person, not just an idea, and I was of course. Myself.

Steve gave me a long, long, searching stare. Then he turned to Martin Dwyer and Gary Talbot, obviously to see what they thought. Martin shrugged, then Gary. They seemed to be getting a bit bored by the whole business of me. They'd really have been happier going round hurting anyone they fancied hurting, only Steve probably didn't let them.

'OK,' Steve said quite mildly, turning back. 'As long as "your best" means one hundred per cent sure, because if it doesn't. . . .' He made a little chop in the air with his hand, the way people do to kill rabbits. Then he added, 'You have been thinking after all, then, haven't you? I don't know why you didn't say so before, 'stead of wasting our time with all that "don't agree" rubbish.'

'Sorry,' I muttered. I was feeling too low to care what I said now.

'Prove it then,' he said.

He wanted to show me that I'd know at once what he meant, and I did. I fumbled in my pocket and held a fifty-pence piece towards him.

'And what's that for?' he asked – again, just to make me say it.

'Bike insurance,' I muttered.

'Louder.'

A wild thought of screaming it so loud that the whole

32

school could hear passed quickly through my mind and out the other side.

'Bike insurance,' I said.

'Say, "I'd like some bike insurance, please".'

'I'd like some bike insurance, please.' I raised the fifty pence towards him again.

'You know I don't take money off people,' he said, looking down at it disgustedly.

As if this was a well-known signal, Martin Dwyer stepped forward, took the money from my fingers and stepped back again, slipping it into his jacket pocket.

'Now say "Sorry for wasting your time",' said Steve.

'Sorry for wasting your time.'

'Louder.'

'Sorry for wasting your time.'

'Yeah, you might yet be,' was his parting shot as the three of them pushed me aside and shambled off out of the office. As they turned the corner out of sight I heard Steve shout a loud, jokey, ''Allo, darling! Give us a kiss' – obviously to one of the crowd of girls in his year who thought he was the best thing since sliced bread.

Hearing it, I felt again that I hated and despised him even more than I was afraid of him. But how could I possibly believe myself after what had just happened?

Perhaps I should have explained a bit better what I'd actually done to draw Steve Mallinson's attention down on me like this.

What he'd been doing – apparently ever since the end of his third year (he was now in the fourth) – was to collect money from nearly every pupil in the school, fifth years included. And the way he'd done it was quite clever – even I had to admit that.

From somewhere – people said it was his uncle or

older brother – he got huge stocks of little books with puzzles and a few jokes and 'interesting facts' in them. They were rubbish: very thin, on cheap paper, weedy-as-hell jokes, and the puzzles couldn't keep a donkey busy for long. As for the facts, they were things like, 'Did you know that in Japan they eat . . . *RAW FISH*!!!' (Actually I did know, because Dad happened to mention it once.) Those books were even worse than the kind of thing that gets given away with cereals or that you find boxes full of, in junk shops – 'LOOK. BARGAIN – ONLY 10p!'

Anyway, the only thing everybody understood clearly was simply that they had to buy one each term at a price of 30p. The books were different every term, so if you couldn't produce the right one when Steve's mates challenged you, then you were in trouble – and that would probably mean you had to buy 'bike insurance' as well, at a cost of 50p, whether you had a bike or not. And if you refused to do that, then you knew you'd be 'done' out of school one day, by Steve's mates outside. That hardly ever happened, though, because the stories about what it was like to be 'done' were so terrifying (like that one about little Darren Williams) that nobody dared to let things go that far. They paid up.

One real beauty of the scheme from Steve's point of view was that because the books were supposed to work like a kind of passport or identity card (you had to write your name on the cover) he didn't have to try to flog them. Come the beginning of term, everyone queued up to buy, and you never felt you could relax till you had one. It was said that there were a few who dared to risk not buying, but only a very few, and of course they didn't go round advertising who they were. I only knew one.

The whole setup worked because nobody was ever sure of anything except the fact that they were scared. It was the stories that did it. I never knew if they were started deliberately by Steve or if they just grew around him.

One story was that the teachers knew all about Steve, but didn't interfere because what he did helped to keep order in the school. People said that a second-year girl had once tried to tell her year tutor about Steve, and she'd been given a detention! The tutor told her it was for trying to get other pupils into trouble – 'for spreading malicious gossip' was how the story had it. Nobody seemed to know exactly which girl or which teacher it had been – or rather, everybody did know, but they all named different ones, which comes to the same thing.

Another story was that Steve had got his outside mates to vandalize the house of some parents who'd tried to make a fuss about it when their son told them what was going on. They'd smashed everything they could and torn everything they couldn't, and done things like putting glue in the beds and weedkiller on the lawn. Again no one knew who exactly.

Another was that Steve had spies everywhere but nobody was sure who they were. They didn't have to pay for their books and they sometimes got little presents as long as they ran and told Steve whenever they heard anyone speaking against him. Sometimes you'd hear kids who didn't like each other, or who'd quarrelled, calling each other 'spy!'

In the end, then, there seemed to be a lot more to be lost than gained by telling on him to parents or teachers.

Apart from the danger of even starting, we felt it would be very hard to find enough evidence against him to get him chucked out of the school, so he'd still be there. And if Steve was still there and anyone had told, his spies would be sure to carry it to his ears who'd done it. Then whoever had told would be 'done'. Against that, 30p a term didn't seem a huge amount to pay.

In fact, as far as I could see, the only danger for Steve's setup was that a group of kids might get organized well enough to all tell together, before he could divide them up and silence them one by one. And that was what I had begun trying very cautiously to do.

I think the main reason I got into trouble was exactly because I'd gone at it so cautiously. I don't know much about fighting, and I don't want to, but I imagine that if you're going to attack a strong enemy, you don't go about it cautiously, otherwise he learns what you're up to and attacks first.

And that was what Steve did. I'd got as far as saying to a few girls I thought I could trust, something like, 'Hey, I don't think this is fair, is it? Paying all this money for something we don't want. Why don't we all get together and refuse?' I suppose I must have said it to the wrong person, or one of the ones I said it to told someone else. Anyway, next thing I knew I was in front of Steve, and that's the bit I've already told you about.

Now, as I left my second interview with Steve, still feeling weak and trembly and very low, I kept turning over and over in my mind what it was I'd actually promised him with the words: 'I'll do my best not to make trouble for you.' Even though she wasn't exactly on my side, Laura had been very determined, when we'd worked it out, that I should not promise anything definite, but it had got to sound as if it was.

'Then if you're stupid enough to change your mind later,' she'd said up there in the Ziggurat, 'and you decide you are strong enough to risk doing something Steve'd call "trouble", you needn't feel guilty about breaking a promise.'

Why on earth anyone should ever feel guilty about breaking anything belonging to that lump of evil muck, let alone a promise forced out of me, I absolutely do not know, but the fact was I was very worried. I felt I'd tied my own hands. What was worse, I felt as if I'd tied my conscience up in a bundle and chucked it away.

Laura : My Ziggurat

Robyn seemed to spend the whole of that week worrying. She kept on and on about it, how it wasn't *fair*, it wasn't *right*, and what was she going to *do*? I listened to her, but kept insisting that the only place to sort those things out was the Ziggurat. The evenings were light now, but we obviously weren't allowed to wander in the Pikestone estate in the evenings, so it had to wait till Saturday afternoon.

She was late, of course. I walked twenty-nine steps away from the Ziggurat, put my coat down on a patch of grass, and sat on it cross-legged like an Indian, facing up towards the top platform.

The thing I loved about the Ziggurat was how it could be both very, very real and also whatever you wanted it to be in your mind. Today, for example, it was an oracle – one of those temples where people used to go to find out what was going to happen to them in the future and what they should do about it. Maybe that's what the ancient ziggurats were actually for, though no one seems quite certain. Anyway, it had to be an oracle today, because Robyn really needed to know.

For Jake the week before, it had been Roman and military, because I knew he needed all that strong stuff about soldiers and fighting. I still wasn't exactly sure why I'd ended up choosing that other story about the husband and the lover, though – maybe because I think that if you have to fight, it can be about other things than nameless soldiers winning battles and controlling people.

Everyone else round here calls the Ziggurat 'the Obelisk', but it isn't an obelisk either. My dad says that it's an eighteenth-century 'folly', and that it was only built by some romantic owner of Pikestone to amuse himself and his visitors. That's an all-right point of view occasionally, but mostly it's not one I like – a gang of red-faced squires with whiskers having a good old guffaw about it. Anyway, all that sort of thing ended when Pikestone Hall got burnt down one night in 1815, after a wild drinking party to celebrate the battle of Waterloo.

In fact, the Ziggurat is only one of the interesting things on the Pikestone estate, which is the strangest place imaginable, and I'm not the only one with different stories to tell about it.

On the top of one hill, for example, there are lots of caves connected by tunnels and passages. They're obviously man-made, not natural, but some say they were used by monks for praying in; others say they were used for torturing people in. One person in the village told me they were used for storing secret weapons during the First World War, but I don't believe that, and he's not old enough to remember it himself anyway.

There are other little caves as well – sort of scooped-out hollows in rock faces – which you come on quite suddenly, and there are several bits of ruins. One bit looks like the remains of a castle, another the remains of a church. Nobody seems to know exactly why or what they were.

There's a couple of old bridges across the very

narrow part of the valley too, though not right across from top to top. One is a stone bridge with no sides to protect you from wandering off it to your probable death. The other, you can't use – a concrete and iron thing that has crashed to the bottom at one end, and is mostly just twisted, rusty metal and chunks of rubble.

Robyn did arrive at last, with her usual apologies, and I said straight away, 'I think this is a matter we're going to have to go right to the top for.'

You see, the Ziggurat has different levels of importance. If it's only chatting and joking and having fun, then outside is good enough, or just inside at the bottom of the stairs when it's raining. Sometimes, though, either me or Robyn has a secret or a problem we want to share, and in that case we have to go up through the darkness to the first window. I call them 'windows' but really they're more like the kinds of slits they had in castles for shooting arrows out of – too narrow even to poke your head right through. You're about level with the tops of most of the trees there, and on a clear day you can just see the Carnwold Hills, all blue in the distance.

From the second window you can see Ashleigh, about five miles away, so this is a good place for talking about little school problems – troubles with teachers and homework and suchlike. It was where Robyn and I had sorted out what she was going to say to Steve next time he got hold of her, because although things had looked more dangerous then, they hadn't seemed to be quite so deeply important for her as I felt they were now. Maybe it had been a mistake only to go that high; maybe we should have gone to the top first time.

The third window is the one that looks out over most of the Pikestone estate, though you can't see the village because it's down in a hollow. Nevertheless, the fact that you know it's out there makes this a good place for complaining about parents, and the things they won't let you do that you want to, and the things you don't want to do that they make you. By this stage the stairs are much cleaner and you can sit on them. You're miles above the trees already, so there are no twigs or leaves except what the birds have dropped, and of course not so much dust to come down from above because there's far less of the Ziggurat above.

The fourth window is the last before the top. The view from here is of sloping fields for miles and miles till you can occasionally believe you're seeing the sea, over fifty miles off. I hadn't yet decided what the fourth window was for, but I was absolutely certain we were going to need it some day for something special.

After that there are twenty-two more stairs to the very top, making one hundred and fifty stairs in all.

Robyn looked quite alarmed when I said we had to go to the top. We had been once or twice, just to look, but we'd never discussed anything that high up. She nodded an unwilling agreement, though, and I led her on up over the dust and dirt.

We held hands round and round and up through the darkness, as we always did, and I didn't let go even when the light from the first window began to brighten. It was as well I didn't, because Robyn tried to pause here, saying, 'I suppose you could think of it as a secret, really,' and I had to tug her up and round past it.

She tried again at the second window. 'It is a school problem, after all, isn't it, like last time?'

'It seems much more than that now,' I said firmly, tugging at her again, even though I was panting quite hard now.

At the third window we simply had to rest to get our breath back, and she took the opportunity to pant out, 'I suppose – huh – you could think of it – huh – as a parent problem too – huh – in a way.'

But she knew it was no good, and she didn't attempt to say anything at the fourth window. Instead it was me that paused there for a moment. Was this the special thing that the fourth window was for? Something told me it wasn't, and I dragged Robyn on up.

You expect to find something to prepare you for the top, but there isn't. The remaining stairs wind on up, and if you're not counting you've no idea where you are. Then you do what turns out to be the last turn, and suddenly above you is a flat bit about a metre long, leading to a smallish doorway which is completely open – no actual door on it. Because you're looking from below, you can of course see nothing but sky through it.

You have still about nine stairs to go, and you do the first four very cautiously, almost tiptoeing, your heart in your mouth. By then your eyes are a fraction above the level of what lies outside the door. From the bottom of the Ziggurat the platform doesn't look so very small, but from the top it looks not much more than a windowsill over the edge of which is nothing but emptiness and death. Two more steps, and beyond this sill you can begin to see the ground, where the big trees are like small bushes, though you can't see anything like directly down to the base or even down into the clearing. You wouldn't ever be able to see the base of the Ziggurat from the top here without going right out on to the platform and leaning over the edge, which only a madman would do.

The first time we came to the top I did manage the final five steps. I even crawled on to the flat bit and poked my head just through the door into the open, but there was no question in my mind of trying to go any further or even standing up. Apart from anything else, Robyn, still determinedly five steps down, was clutching my ankle shouting, 'No, Laura!' and I wasn't too sorry. It's nice to have someone stopping you from having to show you daren't go on, then nobody – not even you yourself – knows how much of a coward you really are. Because unless you're absolutely determined to kill yourself you've got to stop *some*where, and does it desperately matter exactly where?

Robyn herself stopped on the fifth-from-the-top step that time, and only shook her head violently when I asked if she wanted to try the last part with me holding on to her.

By the way, I've forgotten to mention the wind. However still it is below, the wind always seems to blow up here, roaring in little gusts round the top of the Ziggurat, making it tremble ever so slightly.

Today we had more important things than proving how brave we were, so without thinking of trying to go any further I sat myself down on the third step from the top and Robyn sat on the fifth. There was a pause while our breathing came back to normal – silence, except for that and the wuthering of the wind outside.

'Right,' I said briskly as soon as I could. 'Now what really *is* the problem? Steve's not on your back any longer, you've got no more meetings with him to face, but you're even more upset than you were at half term.'

'I just feel so bad, Laura. I keep not understanding why I gave in like that. And I know I've absolutely *got* to do something about it.'

'You mean you'd be happier if you were still feeling scared of being attacked in Ashleigh, or meeting Steve again, or a load of thugs coming out to the village on motorbikes to duff your parents up?'

'No, I – yes. In a way, yes. No. I don't *know*!'

'Look,' I said. 'You know I don't agree with you and I think you can't possibly win. I just don't understand why you can't stop bothering with it all.'

'Because I can't.' She was suddenly quite angry. 'It isn't right, and what *I* don't understand is how things ever got like this – how people let them.'

She was staring at me accusingly. I was about to say that it wasn't *my* fault, but decided not to waste my breath. From Robyn's point of view it *was* my fault, in a way – me and hundreds of others like me, too lazy or too scared to lift a finger. But I also knew this thing she couldn't seem to grasp. Even if she'd been as big and tough and old as Steve himself, he had power and she hadn't. There was just something about him that made other people want to obey him, and no amount of arguing or being right would change that.

I tried to put it in a way she could understand. 'You can't go straight at him, Robyn. You'll get hurt, and you'll probably get others hurt too.'

'So you're just saying "Give up" again.'

'No, I'm saying you've – I mean *we've* got to do it in a roundabout way. If he's got the magic of power, we've got to use the magic of cunning.'

She pulled a sour face. 'Oh, magic.'

'No, forget magic then. Cunning.'

'I think that's sneaky. It's no better than he is.'

'Well, according to you, giving in to him's no better than he is, either. What *do* you want to do?'

'I want people to see sense. I want everybody to see what's really happening and how bad it is.'

A gust of wind echoed round the Ziggurat and blew a

little draught down on us through the open doorway.

'How about a newspaper then?' I said suddenly.

'Eh? Start a newspaper? But nobody'd –'

'Not start one yourself, stupid, use one that's there already. Use the *Ashleigh Chronicle*. It'd be a good story for them, and you wouldn't have to say who you were. Write a letter to them and don't sign it.'

'But that's –'

'Sneaky, yes. But it could work. Anyway it's not that sneaky. All you'll have done is tell them there *is* a story. You don't even have to tell them it's about Steve, only *what* it's about. They'll send someone to find out the facts, and Steve wouldn't dare attack a reporter.'

'But they wouldn't be interested at the *Chronicle*. They only do who's married who, and how the Ashleigh Lions keep losing eighteen-nil.'

'Look,' I said very firmly, getting up to go. 'Do you want to sit there making difficulties or do you want to get off your bottom and do something. Anyway, the Ziggurat's not going to tell us any more today.'

She got up and started to lead the way down, complaining, 'Why do you always have to say that sort of thing – the Ziggurat telling you and so on? It makes it seem like a lucky guess, not really thought out.'

I particularly didn't want to argue with her about that one again, because I myself had an uneasy feeling about the suggestion I'd made to her up there. It wasn't at all the kind of thing I normally got from the Ziggurat. So all I said was, 'Because that's how it is. Let me go first.'

Going down the Ziggurat is good fun if you do it as fast as you dare, trusting your nerve as you plunge right on down through the dark part. Robyn always has to slow up there, of course, and you can't overtake so it's no good her going first.

I had to wait at least a minute for her, out in the sunlight at the bottom. As I did so, I thought what a pity it was that I wouldn't ever be able to make her understand what Steve was really like.

A picture from a story I'd once read passed across my mind. There'd been a King of Dark Magic who cast around him a pool of such utter darkness that it swallowed up anyone who came in its shadow. Those who tried to defeat the King became invisible to each other as soon as they entered his darkness, so that they could not help one another in the fight and he slew them man by man. One person alone, the Knight of Black Wrath, cast an even stronger shadow. When he went into the shade of the King of Dark Magic his men could still see him, even darker, leading them to victory.

Robyn might have blackish hair, I thought, as she finally appeared in the entrance and came towards me, but she's no Knight of Black Wrath.

Jake : Getting In

By the time a week had gone by after that terrible first day, I was at least beginning to get the hang of how the school worked, but I couldn't imagine I was ever going to like it. It was much bigger than my other school, but nearly all one-storey buildings, so it seemed to spread in all directions like a maze.

The thing I hated most, though, was having to wear a uniform, because I'd never had to before. It was mostly grey, with a white shirt and a stripey school tie. If you wore a jacket it had to be black, but my dad hadn't been able to afford one yet, just a grey pullover. It was the same for girls too, only grey skirts instead of grey trousers. I kept remembering the bright colours back home – boys in check shirts, girls in blue jeans and red, pink, yellow sweaters.

Most of all I was lonely. Being big, I was pretty good at football, and that had already helped quite a lot to get me noticed and liked by some of the other lads. But I had nothing approaching the friends I'd had in my other school, nor could I see much chance of it here.

Living so far out was part of the problem. Even though that had been the same in the other school, I'd moved up there together with a gang of us lads from the same village – and that meant we all went to and fro on the same bus, and saw each other at weekends and in the holidays, and so on. Robyn and Laura weren't exactly much substitute, and in any case they were always so deep in their little secrets together that I hadn't done any more than nod 'Hi' to them since that first day.

What I missed even more was what I used to call my 'adventure playground'. The owners of the estate Dad worked for then told him I could have the use of a small field to play in as long as we didn't frighten the horse. It was a fantastic field because it was on a slope, *and* had two little hillocks in it, so it made a terrific place for scrambling and mountain biking and stunts and whatever. (The horse, by the way, turned out to be as frightenable as a heap of sand.) And in the middle of the field there was a thicket of trees round and down into a hollow. We'd been allowed to build dens there, camp there, put swing-ropes up, make mud slides down the banks of the hollow. . . . I wanted to be back in that field alongside the gang I used to whoop around it with – *my* gang.

Because I was lonely at Ashleigh High, I found I'd start talking about those good old days to anyone who'd listen – building it all up a bit, as you do. The field became quite a lot bigger, the gang grew in number, the things we did were more dangerous, more exciting. At first the other lads seemed interested, but then they began to ask questions as if they didn't believe what I was saying.

(Me) '. . . so we stretched this rope right across the hollow for a tightrope, and this lad James –'

'What sort of rope was it?' (That was Stuart Jones, one of those really brainy types.)

'What d'you mean "what sort"?'

'Well, it'd have to be a really strong sort of rope to

48

stretch right across that length *and* hold someone's weight.'

'Yeah, well, it was a wire rope.'

'Crikey! Bit difficult to keep your footing on that, wasn't it?'

And so on. You see what I mean, though. The fact was that me and the gang had only talked about putting a rope across, and Stuart was quite right in what he thought – we'd given up because there'd been no chance of getting one that would do. Stuart didn't say so, but I could see he was taking my story with a large pinch of salt.

The result was that I still found myself alone far too much of the time. Breaktimes dragged, and I was glad to get back into lessons. Me, glad to get back into lessons!

It was one break around the beginning of the second week when I was walking along going nowhere in particular, looking down at the tarmac, kicking at bits of twig and pebbles, that I suddenly became aware I was going to bump into somebody if I didn't change direction. I looked up to see those two fourth-years who'd stopped Robyn on that first day. They were standing blocking my path, and when I turned aside, the short hefty one stepped to block that direction too. So I stopped. There didn't seem much else for me to do.

It was the other one who spoke. 'You new here?'

'Yes, I –'

'What's your name?'

'Jake – Jake Hetherington.'

'You got a book yet?'

'A book? They gave me some exercise books, but –'

The two of them looked at each other, rolled their

49

eyes as though to say 'We've got a right one here', then sniggered.

'He doesn't even know!' said the heavy one.

'He doesn't even know who his own dad is,' crowed the thin one.

'Nor does his mum,' the other answered, as if it was a set routine.

I couldn't follow what was going on. For a split second I wondered if they actually knew about my mum and were trying to upset me on purpose. But then I thought they couldn't know – it was just some regular joke of theirs. The thin one was holding a little book out at me that he'd fished from his jacket pocket. It had a gaudy cartooned cover and I could just catch the title, *Bumper Fun Book*.

'This is what we mean by a book,' he was saying.

'It's thirty pence,' said the heavy one, holding his hand out at me. 'And write your name on the cover.'

I took the book and opened it. It was about the size of a cassette, only thinner – just a couple of pages stapled inside, typed not printed, with a bad drawing or two and some little jokes or something. '*What hurts when you look through it? A window pain [pane]*.' Even at a first glance I could see it wasn't worth thirty pence, though that was what the price ticket on the cover said, and in any case I hate those kinds of books.

'No thanks,' I said, handing it back. I could of course see that they were putting pressure on me, but I couldn't see any danger – not here, in the school playground. That may sound stupid to you, but don't forget I wasn't used to any kind of bullying. In any case, I fancied myself as big and tough for my age – I always had been, compared with others.

Instead of taking the book, the thin one put his hands

behind his back so that he couldn't, and smiled a thin, hard smile.

'We don't want it,' he said. 'It's *you* that wants it.'

'No I don't,' I said. I put the book down on the ground.

The thin one looked at it, then up at me, then at his mate in amazement.

'He really doesn't know, does he?' he said.

'No, he wants telling.'

As he said that, the heavy one moved, so casually that I was caught totally off guard. He reached out and grabbed at my tie, yanking it out of my pullover, twisting it round his hand, pulling quickly forward and down, all in one well-practised movement. Even if I'd dared – and I don't believe I would have – I couldn't use my hands to hit him or fend him off because I was falling forward and needed them to stop my face meeting the ground first.

Next thing I knew, I was helpless on my hands and knees on the tarmac in front of him, staring straight down at his heavy black toecaps, still not able to lift a hand to help myself because he had this grip on my tie and could easily jerk me off balance.

'*Now* he's beginning to learn,' came the smooth voice of the thin one. 'OK, pick up the book.'

His foot pushed it over to within my reach. Unsteadily I put my hand out and clutched at it. There didn't seem anything else to do till I could get out of my present position.

'Good,' the smooth voice came again. 'Now if you reach ever so carefully back into your pocket, you might be able to get us the money to pay for it.'

'I haven't got any money,' I tried, for no really good

reason – just playing for time, just desperate to put off giving in completely.

My tie was tugged so violently that I nearly toppled forward on my nose. At the same time I became aware that the thin one was behind me, patting at my trouser pockets. I heard the two fifty-pence coins Dad had given me for my dinner clink together.

'You're gonna wind up in trouble, you are,' said the heavy one. He gave three little jerks on the tie to accompany the words, 'Get – it – out.'

I put my hand back, took one of the coins out, then suddenly couldn't resist throwing it a little way in front of me. Next thing I knew, I was dragged forward almost to lying flat, with my nose right over the coin. I didn't wait to be told to pick it up again. I held it out to them as best I could.

'We like to feel it's given freely,' said the thin one, taking the coin, 'without any undue pressure.' I heard him snigger at his own joke. 'OK, you can let him up now. I think he understands.'

The heavy one unwound my tie from his hand and let go. I got to my feet.

'Your book,' said the thin one, pointing at the ground where I'd left it.

I bent and picked it up without a word, stuffing it angrily into my trouser pocket. 'Don't I get any change?'

'I think not,' said the thin one. He gave a huge false smile showing black fillings in his side teeth. 'Because of the extra trouble you've given us. We can put it towards your bike insurance, which you're certainly going to need.'

He turned and started to walk away. The heavy one turned to follow, not looking at me, but saying lazily, half over his shoulder, 'Write your name on the cover like I said, case we meet you again.'

I stood there, letting them walk away, letting the anger boil up inside me to reckless bursting-point. Then I ran. I ran straight for the heavy one's back, jumped on it, arm round his neck, throwing my weight backwards hard. He crashed back over on top of me, arms and legs thrashing about, but I had him under the chin, with my other hand gripping hold of my wrist like mad.

I felt the thin one now, kicking me in my side, hissing at me, 'You bloody moron!' but I didn't care. There wasn't much he could do while I held his mate like that. Besides, I could hear footsteps, little cries of 'Fight! Fight!', see legs running towards us. People were coming to stop us.

Then suddenly everything went still. The kicking died down. The body on top of me seemed to have given up struggling though it was still panting hard. The running legs had stopped moving. There was almost silence except for a single set of footsteps coming closer. I heard a strong, firm voice.

'OK. What's goin' on?'

I thought I knew for certain what it was. A teacher had arrived on the scene, maybe even the Head. It was safe to let go, and I slowly relaxed my grip on my wrist and unhooked my arm from under the chin. We both scrambled untidily to our feet and I looked around, dazed.

But there didn't seem to be a teacher – only that Steve I'd seen talking to Robyn, facing us, angry. He opened his mouth to say something to us, but then instead turned sharply round on the onlookers.

'Clear off, you lot. There's nothing for you to see here.'

To my surprise everyone just melted away, dis-appearing round the corners of buildings, till there were only the four of us left. The heavy one was still red-faced and panting; the thin one was kicking sulkily at the ground; I was just plain bewildered. Only Steve seemed sure of himself.

'Gary, Martin – before we deal with this kid, I want to know what happened.' Then to me, 'You wait here.'

The three of them strolled a few steps away – far enough for me not to be able to hear more than the mutter of their irritated voices. I stood there alone, considering whether to make a run for it, but I decided it wasn't worth it. They'd only get me some other time.

I watched the pair explaining to Steve. I now knew the thin one was Martin – he seemed to be doing most of the talking. His hands were going wild as he talked. He seemed to be arguing against Steve, protesting. Gary was standing looking from one to the other, only speaking when he was asked a question.

You can imagine I was nervous – even frightened – about what was going to happen to me, which was why I was so anxiously watching the other two, wondering what they were saying about me. But more and more I found the person I couldn't take my eyes off was Steve.

It wasn't only that I suppose you could call him good-looking in an actor sort of way – jet black hair, eyebrows and eyes, and a skin tanned dark enough to make his shirt seem dazzling. No, the main thing about Steve is simply the way he always looks so totally in command of whoever he's speaking to, even if he isn't really. He just holds himself that way, moves that way. When later I happened to see him talking to a teacher, it was still the same: Steve looked as if he was the teacher, the teacher as if he was the pupil.

54

Eventually Steve nodded, then came over to me, giving the other pair a little movement of his hand that told them to stay where they were. He began to ask me questions about where I'd come from, not rudely but firmly, as if he didn't expect me for one second not to answer or tell the truth. Then he asked me who my friends were and I said I hadn't got any yet, except that I lived near Laura and Robyn.

At this, he stared at me thoughtfully for a few seconds and said, 'I wouldn't have much to do with that Robyn if you've got any sense.' Then he strolled back to the other two for a quick word. This time it was Gary who seemed to be protesting. When he'd quietened down, Steve beckoned me over to join them. For some reason I was feeling far less nervous now.

'He wants you done,' Steve said calmly to me, pointing at Gary. 'But I think you only did what you did because you're new here. That right?'

I nodded. In a way it was true, what he'd said.

'And you're very sorry, aren't you?' Steve went on.

This was a bit too much to take, but before I could make a fuss, Steve very skilfully continued, 'And I think you could be useful to us, so I'm gonna ask Gary to forgive you.'

Gary held out his hand, staring at me with no expression at all in his pale eyes. Not knowing what else to do, I shook hands with him. His face remained expressionless.

'What's more,' said Steve, 'we're gonna give you this back.'

He held out the fifty-pence piece. I took it, then began to pull the book out of my pocket, but Steve motioned me to stop.

'No, we don't want that back. The other kids'll think

there's something funny going on if you don't have one. But we do have a problem.'

He was talking to me now as if I was one of them – same level, same age. Even though I was still unsure and a bit suspicious, I couldn't help feeling my head getting bigger. Me, with them!

'Yeah,' Steve was saying. 'Trouble is, too many people saw you with Gary down on the floor . . .'

I didn't dare look at Gary, but kept my eyes firmly fixed on Steve's face.

'. . . and there's two things about that. Nobody's got to be seen to get Gary down and not pay for it, or it makes things very hard for him, and the other thing is you'll be no use to us if people think we let you off.'

Gary said, 'We could do him over just a bit.' I still didn't dare catch his eye, but I could see his big fists clench and unclench at his sides.

Martin gave a nasty little laugh. 'I don't think this Jake kid would go for that. That's if we really wanna use him.'

'We do,' said Steve firmly. 'He's big and he's a loner and we like him.'

'Tell you what,' I found myself saying. 'I'm pretty bruised on my back as it is. Why don't I just say you gave me a kick up the backside and took all my money off me? I can do without dinner today.' The distant sound of the end-of-break bell from inside the main building added a thought. 'And there wasn't time to do more 'cos the bell went.'

'Mm . . . maybe.'

'And I could say I still don't know what's gonna happen to me, as well.'

'OK,' said Steve, starting to lead the way. 'Leave it like that for now. But stick around in case we want you, or in case we change our minds. Now get lost.'

I obediently left them to go to my classroom. The main thought in my head was how lucky I'd been and how exciting things were looking. Being the baby of a gang when I'd been used to leading my own may not sound much to get excited about, but these people were as hard as you could get in this school, I reckoned. Besides, even though I couldn't exactly say I liked him, this Steve seemed to be a fantastic person.

Robyn: Help from Above?

This was the letter I sent.

To the Editor of the Ashleigh Chronicle

Dear Sir or Madam,

I am writing to you because of a problem we have at our school, Ashleigh High School. I do not want to tell you any names because I do not think it is right to do that, and I am hoping that you will send somebody to investigate it and write a story in your newspaper to show what is happening.

One of the boys in the fourth year is making the pupils at the school buy books they do not want and which are not worth the money, and if they do not buy the books he makes them pay extra for bike insurance, which only means that you get your bike damaged if you have one and do not pay. Anyone who dares to try and tell on him can get beaten up by his friends who do not go to the school, which is why I dare not sign my name on this letter.

Please will you send a reporter to the school to find out what is going on. My friends and I will be very grateful if you can do something.

Yours sincerely,
A First-Year Pupil

For several days after I'd posted it I watched every stranger I saw come into the school, thinking, 'That must be him! That must be her!' Every day I expected to see someone asking questions in the playground, or to hear one of my friends say they'd been approached.

In fact nothing happened till the middle of the week after, when I was in class doing a French exercise. I remember exactly what that exercise was, because it was just as I was trying to translate into English, '*Est-ce qu'elle est méchante?*' that the classroom door opened and the secretary came in, whispered something to our French teacher, then announced, 'The Head would like to see Robyn Somers now.'

Of course everyone went 'Ooooh!' at me as I staggered to my feet, but it was made such a lot worse by this translation I'd just done, whirling round in my brain: '*Is she naughty?*' My stomach must have done at least seven somersaults and I could hardly keep a straight line following the secretary down to the Head's office, wondering what on earth I'd done. Naturally I didn't connect it with my letter because there was no reason to.

Not that the Head seems all that frightening, though I'd never spoken to him before. Dad only ever calls him 'that soulless administrator', which sounds about right, even if I'm not sure what it means exactly. Mr Dunning is small and thin, with glasses and neat grey hair, and always wears different shades of grey suits. In fact the only surprising thing about him is that he has a deep, strong voice, which sounds odd coming out of that body.

The secretary showed me straight in. Mr Dunning was sitting there behind his desk and in the corner a bit behind him was another man I didn't know. He was a big man with straggly grey hair and untidy-looking clothes, and his raincoat was folded over his knees as if he'd just come or was just going. Mr Dunning pointed to the chair opposite his desk, so I sat down in it, still desperately trying to think what it could all be about – what I was supposed to have done.

'I'll come straight to the point, er, Robyn,' said the Head, pulling a sheet of paper out of a folder in front of him. 'Did you write this?'

He held it up. It was my letter to the *Ashleigh Chronicle*.

I'd be a liar if I pretended that the thought of lying didn't cross my mind for a moment. Anyway, I must have hesitated just a bit, because the next thing Mr Dunning said sounded like a kind of warning.

'I should tell you that we've checked the handwriting – against your school work. That was how we arrived at your name as the probable author.'

'Yes,' I said. 'It was –'

'Well, at least you admit it, and at least your English isn't too shaming to the school.' He half turned to the man in the corner, with his lips in a thin smile that vanished when he turned back in my direction. 'Mr Pilkington sent it straight to me, of course.'

I understood that Mr Pilkington must be the man in the corner, and that he must be something to do with the *Chronicle* – maybe the Editor. What I didn't understand was why the Head said 'of course'. The whole point of the letter had been that it was for the newspaper and *not* for anyone in the school to see.

Half a hope sprang up in me, that perhaps it was because everything had been sorted out without me knowing. Perhaps a reporter had been and found out the whole story, and now they'd brought me in to thank me! But the hope died when I started to pay attention to the Head again.

'You must surely realize,' he was saying, sounding quite cross now, 'that we simply cannot have pupils at this school writing to the local newspaper to complain about the way the school is run. Certainly not before they've explored every avenue of complaint available in the school.'

Again I didn't really understand what he was on about. There weren't any 'avenues of complaint' in the school. There was running to tell tales to a teacher, and that was it. Even if you didn't feel it was wrong to do that – and I did – nobody would be so stupid as to run and tell tales about Steve.

'But since you chose to go about things in this underhand way, I naturally had to ask Mr Pilkington to come along' – half-turn, thin smile again – 'and he's an extremely busy man – so that he could see for himself that we have absolutely nothing to hide here. Now what exactly is your complaint?'

I must just have sat there looking bewildered, because he had to ask me again.

'What exactly is the problem?'

'It's – er – it's what it says in the letter, Mr Dunning.'

'I see.' He picked up the letter and skimmed through it carelessly, as if he'd already forgotten what was in it and wasn't really bothered.

'So who is this fourth-year boy who seems, as far as I can gather, to be guilty of extortion, blackmail, criminal assault and heaven knows what else? Enough to send him to jail for several years, I should think, if half of it was to be believed.'

With that last bit, the whole truth suddenly burst on me. The Head wasn't a bit concerned to find out what was really happening. He only wanted to show this

Pilkington man that there *wasn't* anything going on – that my letter was a load of lies.

That meant I had two choices. Either I just gave up and let the Head have his way, or I had to produce some facts to prove that what I'd said had something to it.

'Well? Who is he?'

Still I hesitated. I must have looked like a frightened rabbit, sitting there, saying nothing.

'I see. Imagination went a bit wild, did it?' Then he leant over towards me with a smile that was meant to look kind, and said in a much softer voice, 'Look, Robyn, if you're at all worried about speaking out, you must surely know that anything you do say will be entirely between us. Isn't that so, Mr Pilkington?'

Mr Pilkington nodded and said, 'Yes, if you really are frightened, you've no need to be. We won't breathe a word – cross my heart and hope to die.'

He grinned, doing the actions little kids do as he said it, and I instantly hated and distrusted him. Here was the man who'd sent my letter to him straight to someone else, asking me to believe that he wouldn't repeat anything I said. He had a nerve, he had!

So I went on sitting in silence, looking down at my knees.

'You may think it's wrong to tell tales, Robyn,' said Mr Dunning. 'But really it isn't. If anybody, be they pupil or teacher, is doing something bad, it is they who are wrong, not the people who inform on them. We are on your side, Robyn, and *if* there's anyone who wants to hurt you, then he is *not* on your side.'

How could I possibly explain that I didn't trust them – that I was even more worried about the danger from their big mouths than about the wrongness of telling tales?

62

'After all,' said Mr Pilkington, 'none of my reporters would ever be able to find out the truth about your claim if everybody behaved like you, not telling them things they need to know.'

For one wild second my tongue was desperate to blurt out, 'Steve Mallinson,' just to show him. But it didn't. I controlled it.

In fact everything was hopeless. All I wanted to do now was to give them what they were after and get out of there. And I had no doubt what they were after. The Head wanted me to say in front of Mr Pilkington that there wasn't a word of truth in my letter, so that the name of his school could be kept nice and clean, and Mr Pilkington wanted the same because he was afraid of offending the Head. They wanted me to brush my own dirt under the carpet where it wouldn't be seen, but they didn't want me to understand that.

'I'm sorry, I can't tell you any more,' was all I could finally manage to come out with.

But that wasn't enough, apparently. 'When you say "can't",' Mr Dunning said carefully, 'do you mean because you don't know any more than you've written here, or because you don't want to say – because you're frightened to speak out, as you claim?'

'I don't know,' I said. Of course I only meant it the way you do to teachers and people when you don't know what to say, but the moment it was out of my mouth, he jumped on it with the meaning *he* wanted it to have.

'So you are really not able to tell us any more?'

Well, that was true too in another sense, and I'd given up anyway, so I said, 'No.'

'In that case,' he said, 'we needn't waste any more of Mr Pilkington's valuable time over a nonexistent storm in an imaginary teacup.'

He got up, smiling, and so did Pilkington. I started to get up, but he waved his hand at me to tell me to stay where I was, then began to show Pilkington out, saying to him, 'I shall of course try to sort out exactly what was going on in this girl's mind, but I needn't trouble you with that. I'm only sorry that you've had to . . .'

Their voices went on as they moved out into the secretary's office, but I couldn't hear what they were saying. As if I cared. The big worry that was now beginning to surface in my mind was the fact that all my class had seen me being taken to see the Head. What was I going to say to them? And far worse, what was Steve going to say – or do – when *he* heard from someone, as he surely would?

Mr Dunning came back in, looking as if he'd been busy wiping that false smile completely off his face. He didn't sit, but stood beside his desk, glaring down at me.

'I don't think I need to say how angry I am about this.'

He was right – he didn't need to say. His usually pale face was almost brick-red.

'You write some cock-and-bull piece of a scandal story off to our local newspaper, dragging the name of this school in the mud – anonymously too – and when challenged you say in effect that there isn't a word of truth in it.'

Don't think I didn't want to defend myself. I did, desperately. But my only defence was to make him believe the full story. If I once started to tell and he didn't believe it, or only half believed it and started 'investigating' in his ham-fisted way, I'd be in terrible danger. I didn't dare risk it.

So I had to let him go on telling me off, threatening

me with this and that punishment. And of course the longer I sat there taking it without protesting, the more certain he was that I was as guilty of making the whole thing up as he wanted to believe.

By the time he allowed me to go he'd called me a liar, a trouble-maker, a person who'd do anything to attract attention to herself and stupid. He'd also managed to suggest that I was a freak and perhaps a bit touched – 'anyone in their right mind,' he kept saying, over and over.

Yet when he finally opened the door into the secretary's office to boot me out, and she was there at her desk, do you know what he did?

He put his hand on my shoulder and said in a fatherly sort of way, 'Anyway, Robyn, in spite of my being understandably a little annoyed on this occasion, I'm sure you do know that if you have any *real* troubles ever, I'd be the first person to listen sympathetically to them.'

I think I'd always vaguely felt till then that lying was something which children did but which you simply grew out of as you got older. It had never occurred to me that you might actually get better at it!

Laura :
Thoughts of Various Kinds

Here's something I wrote in my Thoughtbook around this time. I hadn't kept a diary after the first two months' experimenting when I was nine. (You know – '*Got up 7.30. Went to school. Did English first, I got 9 out of 10 for my homework!!!*' etc.) Instead, when Dad gave me an old book of blank lined pages with a hard cover he'd dug out from somewhere in the depths of one of the post office drawers, I decided to keep a thoughtbook. Daily things were so boring to write down; thoughts might be more interesting.

As it happens they mostly weren't. Looking at the book now, it's got far too many Deep Thoughts like,

I wonder if I will ever be able to make a crème caramel as beautifully as my mother does. Mmmm!!!

and

I think maybe Jenny (that was another friend at junior school I used to think was my best friend when Robyn wasn't) *is getting to be fonder of Sue than she is of me. I shall put the evil eye on Sue next time I see her against the sky.*

(I had this thing about seeing people 'against the sky'. If I could get to see them only surrounded by sky I would have power over them. It led me into some odd

66

scrapes, like the time I was found in the primary school yard, lying on the tarmac just so that I could catch big James Hurley, who'd been teasing me, against the sky when he came to the top of the steps. I had a job explaining *that* without giving the secret of my magic away!)

The thoughts that are more interesting are those I had about Steve and Robyn and – later – Jake, around that time. And, of course, about the Ziggurat. This one is from some time early in that June:

Steve Mallinson is a wizard, a black wizard.

His shadow falls everywhere about him, confusing those who would unite against him.

He knows his power, but does not know that it reaches like a wizard's power. Only I know that. He believes he is powerful because he is tough and hard and clever. Maybe he is those things, but they are not why he is powerful.

If he is beaten in the ordinary world, his power will live to grow again. But if his wizardry is broken, his power will leave him for ever.

The key lies in the True Voice of the Ziggurat!

That last one tells me that all those Deep Thoughts were probably brought about by the utter failure of my suggestion that Robyn should write to the *Ashleigh Chronicle*. If only I'd listened properly at the time, I'd have known it was the empty noise of the wind and not the voice of the Ziggurat bringing the idea to me. But Robyn was being too demanding and I was too keen to help her, and so I deceived myself, coming out with that Robyn-type suggestion instead of really concentrating and listening for the True Voice. Yet she's so good-natured she never accused me at all of giving her bad advice. In fact, it didn't seem as if the idea that I might be to blame even crossed her mind.

Up in the top of the Ziggurat she told me about her interview with the Head. Indeed, I was quite surprised at how this time it was Robyn who led the way right up there before she said anything. Then, with her on the fifth step, me on the seventh, it all came out.

It was also typical of Robyn that the thing which worried her most of all was the lie she'd told to her classmates when she came back from seeing the Head.

'I had to, Laura,' she said, 'but now it's yet another thing for me to feel bad about. And what's more, I'm scared stiff that Mr Dunning's going to say something to someone, so I'll have just as much danger as if I'd never lied *and* everyone'll know I did lie to them.'

'So what did you actually say?'

'Oh, I just said he'd wanted to see me about arranging a visit by some of the teachers to the Pikestone Pottery.'

'Robyn!' It wasn't that I was shocked that she'd lied, of course, but I was surprised by what a neat little lie it was. I hadn't known she could do it that well.

'I know, it was awful of me,' she said. 'But what am I going to do now, anyway? Nothing's changed a jot, except that I've probably put myself in even more danger. That Jake seems to have joined up with them now. Maybe he's a spy, only he's not hiding it very well if he is. Well, on Thursday when you were off sick, I went to sit next to him on the bus back, and do you know what he said?'

'Was it, "Get away from me – you stink"?'

'I'm deadly serious, Laura. He just looked up at me and said cold as anything, "I'm keeping away from you."'

'So what did you say?'

'Nothing. I just went and sat somewhere else. But

there's no one who'd have told him to keep away from me except Steve Mallinson, is there?'

'Except me.'

'Be *serious*, Laura. You know I can't stand you when you're in a jokey mood. Specially not when I'm in a panic about something real.'

Then suddenly the feeling got too much for her, and her voice changed from complaining to very near tears.

'You don't seem to understand, Laura! If any word gets to Steve about that letter, I could get badly beaten up. I could get killed, or lose an eye, or something as horrible as that. It happens, Laura, it's real!'

I shan't ever forget the distress on that face looking down into mine, eyes wide open, tears ready to flow. And the reason I shan't forget it is that something began to change in me then. I'd been being jokey because I was afraid of getting drawn again into Robyn's way of seeing things and making another mistake for her. But now suddenly the voice of the Ziggurat was there inside me, telling me that the shadow of Steve Mallinson had got to be lifted, not only from Robyn but from all of us, and that I would have to play my part in doing it.

At first it didn't give me any idea what part. I sat there, staring up at Robyn, not speaking, letting my mind go blank, waiting. Mixed in with the rushing of the wind around us there now came a little pattering noise from the platform and roof above – it was obviously starting to rain out there. For some unknown reason the picture of Jake came into my mind – Jake, sitting alone in a double seat in the bus, shaking his head at Robyn.

Jake was new. Jake was alone and sad. Most of all, Jake knew the Ziggurat and seemed ready to respect it. Yet we'd let him fall under Steve's spell, and every day he was falling deeper and deeper. Even if I could get him out from under it, he couldn't ever fight Steve directly. But perhaps he could. . . . What could he do? The picture was fading –

'Please,' said Robyn.

'There's a chance I can help you, Robyn, and I'm going to try urgently because it *is* urgent. But I'm going to do it my way, not yours, so it's no good me telling you what I'm going to do.'

She looked at me as if she longed to believe me, yet couldn't quite. But rather than show she doubted me, all she asked was, 'So what do *I* do?'

'You just stay out of trouble for the moment. That's the best thing you can do.'

'But what if Mr Dunning says something? I mean, suppose they don't *let* me stay out of trouble.'

'Suppose, what if, and perhaps!' I snapped back. 'Suppose the Ziggurat fell down now? What if Steve and his thugs started coming up the stairs? You're OK for now. If anything new happens, we'll just have to think again quickly. Mind out of the way, I want to look at the rain. I've never seen it in rain.'

I pushed past her and began to crawl up to the threshold of the doorway. I felt her clutch my ankle and was glad of her there, stopping me.

The stone of the platform was wet and shining. Down below, the leaves on the tops of the trees were shining too.

'It's going to be all right,' I shouted back over my shoulder. 'I know it is. I just don't know how, yet.'

Jake : Getting On

For a day or two after Steve had first shown an interest in using me, very little happened. I went to find him once or twice where I'd seen him with Robyn – which I discovered later was called his office – to ask him if there was anything I could do.

The great thing about the office is that it isn't only private, but the way to it isn't used too much and has a lot of turnings-off between different blocks of the school. So nobody can tell for sure that it's the office you're going to if you wander off in that direction. Then when there's no one about on the path, you can do a quick dive between two of the disused mobile classrooms and there you are. Add to that the fact that not many people want to find Steve unless he wants them to, and you'll see why it isn't so difficult to keep it secret that you're working for him.

He didn't have anything at all for me to do to begin with, except keep my eyes and ears open for any signs of trouble, but he did explain a bit how his scheme worked.

Then he gave me my first job. It was a lad in my year – same tutor group as Robyn, in fact – who'd been caught without a book and had already been told he'd got to have bike insurance as well, so he owed 80p. The trouble was he was one of those kids who are always absent from school with some disease or other, and he

71

was sly with it, so it wasn't so easy for Steve to pin him down. His name was Philip Crowther.

'I know he's not the only one that hasn't got a book,' Steve said to me, 'but he's one we've caught, so if we don't chase him up we're in dead trouble.'

Steve also told me that next term he was going to make sure nobody escaped. He wanted someone in each year to be responsible for keeping a proper list, and I'd be doing the second-year list for him.

Anyway, I caught up with this Philip Crowther during an art lesson one Tuesday morning because we happened to be in the same group for art, though he'd not been at school on art days yet. I managed to get myself working at the same double table as him, so it was easy for me to talk to him without anyone noticing anything odd going on. Of course he had no reason to suspect I wanted to be other than friendly.

'You owe Steve Mallinson eighty pence,' I began straight away, speaking normally as if we were just chatting.

'How do you know?' He looked scared immediately.

'Because he asked me to collect it for him.'

'He didn't.'

'Oh yes he did. And by the way, Steve also told me to tell you that if you so much as breathe a word – if anyone in this school gets to hear – that I'm working for him, you'll get done.'

That convinced him, but he still wasn't going to give in.

'I haven't got it on me,' he said.

'So what are you doing for dinner?'

'I bring my own food. I'm on a special diet. My mum and dad don't let me bring any money in case I buy things I'm not supposed to have.'

'You get pocket money, don't you?'

'No. If there's anything I want that I'm allowed to have, my mum or dad gets it for me.'

This was quite a puzzler, and I went back to my drawing for a while, thinking hard. I was not going to fail on my first mission if I could help it. Then, looking over towards Philip Crowther, I suddenly noticed how flash all his equipment was, from his Nike sports bag to his pencil case bursting with Color-Swap pens. I nodded at the pencil case, saying, 'That's worth a quid or two, isn't it?'

He knew what I meant at once. 'My dad'd kill me if I said I'd lost that.'

'Say it was nicked, then. Not your fault if it's nicked.'

'He'd want to know why I hadn't reported it.'

'Say you have, then, but they can't find it. There's lots of things nicked every week in any school, and your dad knows it.'

'But who could I sell it to?'

He was weakening, and he knew it and I knew it. By the end of the art lesson I'd arranged the sale. By the end of the morning break I was able to go along to the office and place eighty pence in Martin Dwyer's hand (I'd been told never to give money direct to Steve) and say, 'From Crowther.'

Steve gave a little whistle of admiration, and that was all the thanks I needed.

I suppose I maybe did feel a bit bad afterwards about leaning on Philip Crowther, because I remember telling myself that if I hadn't done it someone harder might have, so it would have been worse for him, and that if he didn't want to be leaned on he'd just have to stick up for himself more, and that it wasn't my fault he wasn't strong. That sort of thing.

*

Anyway, meanwhile I was still trying to make other friends too, in my own year. There was a group of three lads who always hung around together that I really wanted to get in with because they were all interesting in different ways. There was Rob Bartlett, who was so mad on football that they said his room was completely papered on all four walls with stickers; Kevin Thomas with the sticky-out ears, who could draw cars better than anyone I've ever seen; and Stuart Jones, who was so brainy that he could finish a maths test while the rest of us were still writing the date.

I hung around them quite a bit, and it seemed as if they were beginning to get used to me, but they hadn't at all accepted me as one of them yet. I tried telling them they ought to cycle out to Pikestone one day and I'd show them around, but it turned out they all knew it quite well anyway. In spite of being officially private, it's a favourite place for Ashleigh people to go for walks.

They'd heard about the incident with Gary Talbot, of course, but they seemed to believe it all right when I told them I'd just been done over a bit and let off because I was new. We didn't ever discuss Steve together – me because I had good reasons not to; them because they weren't interested. I suppose they just paid up for their books at the beginning of term, then forgot about it. At least they didn't seem to suspect me of having anything to do with him.

The only person I nearly gave the game away to was that Robyn. It was stupid of me, but I sensed that she meant real trouble, and after what Steve had said I didn't want her anywhere near me – which could have been difficult with her living in the village, travelling on the same bus and so on. I had to put her off for good, and I did so one day by telling her to clear off when she came to sit by me on the bus. For a minute I thought she suspected something – I didn't know what – but then I decided she didn't. How could she possibly connect me being rude to her with anything to do with Steve Mallinson?

For the same reason – that I didn't want to risk meeting her where she might feel she could be friendly – I hadn't dared go near the Ziggurat again since that first time, though I was itching to get up there. I still felt ashamed at the way I'd panicked going into the dark on the stairs and then lied about it to Laura. I wanted to try it again – perhaps with a torch.

I wondered too why I'd lied to Laura instead of asking her if the stairs were safe and suchlike, because I'm sure she knew I hadn't been to the top. She was odd, Laura was. Why had I done that other bit too – telling her everything about me and my mum when I'd only just met her? Maybe it was because I'd been feeling lonely.

Well, I wasn't now. I'd got the possibility of friends and I'd got the big lads on my side, the hard, tough lads.

At the same time I was missing company at weekends. I'd explored most of the interesting places on Pikestone – the caves, the ruins, and so on – but on your own all you can do is go in, on, or round them, say 'Wow!' to yourself a bit, then think about how good it would be to have someone else to share them with.

I also helped Dad with clearing some of the dead trees and branches away. Being the only worker of any kind on the estate, he was totally alone all day and needed company even more than I did. Since Mum went he'd talked very little, and it was hard going being with him. He'd asked me about school a bit and I'd told him what I could. Naturally I couldn't say anything about the part of school that was most important to me just then –

it could have been dangerous, and he'd have dis-
approved like crazy.

Otherwise we talked mostly about the Pikestone
estate and his work. He said it was the strangest job he'd
ever come across, because he didn't know what he was
actually supposed to do. The owners of the estate were
some bank or other who'd bought it cheap and were
only hanging on to it in case it might get to be more
valuable in the future. They felt there ought to be
someone looking after it, but they hadn't the foggiest
idea what 'looking after it' meant in fact.

Dad knew what it meant if an owner actually wanted
something out of an estate, such as timber, but not
where they didn't seem to want to do anything at all
except own it. So he concentrated mainly on tidying up
and repairing whatever he could. He told me he didn't
even know if he was supposed to keep out all the
trespassers who came there for walks, but he'd decided
not to for the moment.

'As long as they don't do any damage, that's where
my responsibility ends,' he said.

'But what if they hurt themselves on any of those
cliffs or caves or ruins?'

'Well, that's their responsibility,' he said. 'Lord,
people can kill themselves anywhere if they've a mind
to.'

Only two or three days after I'd told Robyn to stay away
from me, though, I decided it was stupid to be hiding
from her – or Laura – any longer. Anyway, I reckoned
that my chances of meeting them were pretty small. So
on the Sunday afternoon I took myself up to the
Ziggurat again, using the easy way this time. I didn't
take a torch with me, after all – I'm not sure why – but I

was careful to leave myself a bit more time for this expedition.

If you come up the easy way, you don't approach the Ziggurat from the side with the door in it. The clearing is sort of egg-shaped, with the Ziggurat at the small end and the entrance facing towards the open area – the way I'd first come to it. This time I was approaching from the side, and that was why it wasn't easy to tell if there was anyone around or not.

I stopped to look and listen before I went out into the open, of course, but it was quite a rough day, and impossible to hear much except the noise the wind was making in the trees and bushes; so seeing nothing, I went on, right up to the side of the square base of the Ziggurat. Then I edged cautiously round towards the front, moving my hands along the damp red stonework to keep myself steady and quiet.

I reached the corner and peered round it. Still nobody. After a long, careful pause I started to continue along the front to the entrance.

'Hello!'

Some day, I swore to myself, I would kill that Laura. I'd recognized her voice at once, so it was nothing like so much of a shock as when she'd caught me there the first time. But it still was a shock, and even more unpleasant was feeling myself doing that ridiculous thing of looking wildly around for where the voice could have come from, like some comedian on telly.

'Up here, stupid.'

She was actually very close – only about a couple of metres away, but above my eye level – standing on top of the base almost above the entrance, leaning calmly back against the round part, gazing down at me, smiling in an amused sort of way.

77

'What were you being so cautious about?' she asked. She sounded dead cheeky.

I gave the best retort I could think of on the spur of the moment. 'Trying to sneak up on trespassers, so that I can report them to my dad. You're the first so far.'

'Well, you're not very good at it. I saw you coming miles off. That's why I got up here. People never look up unless they've a reason to.'

She turned her back on me to lower herself over the edge and climb down to the ground. She did it really neatly too, considering how large she was.

'So,' she said, wiping her dirty hands on her jeans, 'you've come at last, have you?'

'What d'you mean?' I said. 'We didn't –'

'Oh, never mind that. I want to talk to you. Let's go up.'

She led the way towards the entrance with not even a half-turn back, as if there was no doubt at all that I'd follow her, and really there wasn't. Although my mind seemed so full of questions that it was one big question mark, I said nothing at all – just obediently went in after her.

This time there was no need to hesitate when I reached the darkness. I could hear her footsteps going ahead, absolutely regular, though I couldn't help feeling my way against the outer wall with my right hand.

Gradually light began to return from the first of the windows. Laura didn't even pause when she got there, but I stopped to look out. Treetops waving about in the wind and bluish hills beyond. We were quite high already.

She waited for me, but still didn't look back, starting up again the moment I came near. We did the same at the second window, where I saw Ashleigh a long way off with a slight haze of smoke hanging over it, and again at the third. You get a fantastic view of the Pikestone estate from that one, but not the village or my house, which are hidden by rises and falls in the ground and by trees.

All this time the questions were rattling about in my mind, the main one being the worry over how far Laura meant to take me. Was she going to expect me to get out on that platform because I'd said I'd done it already? If so, would I dare? And was that lie what she wanted to talk to me about, or was there something else? And if there was, why were we coming up here?

By the time we got to the fourth window I was too occupied with those thoughts to do more than glance out and get a dizzy feeling. A few more steps and I began to feel gusts of fresh air blowing down on me from above. Then above my head I saw flat stone. The stairs didn't go on any higher; we were nearly at the top. As I turned the last corner and saw the sky through the open doorway, I tried to screw up my courage for whatever might be expected of me now.

Instead, Laura suddenly stopped and sat down on about the third step from the top. I stood a bit lower, getting my breath back, waiting.

After a pause while we both panted at each other and the wind outside kept thumping at the Ziggurat, she said, 'We won't go any further – because you've already been out there, haven't you?' She jerked her thumb towards the doorway.

'Yeah, well, I –'

'Except that you haven't,' she said coolly. 'And in any case that isn't what I wanted to talk to you about, which is, *why are you doing Steve Mallinson's dirty work for him?*'

Laura :
Winning Jake

Jake was as completely thrown as I could possibly have hoped. He opened his mouth twice, staring up at me goggle-eyed, then all he could say was, 'How do you know?'

'I know. But why?'

'Yeah, well I – hey, you won't tell anyone, will you?'

'Of course I won't. I don't want to get myself beaten up.'

'No, well, I wouldn't let that happen.'

I gave him a hard laugh. 'Huh! What makes you think *you*'d have any control over whether I was beaten up or not?'

'But I wouldn't let him.'

'I see. So even supposing – even *if*, he told you in advance he was going to have it done, you think you could just wander up to him and say, "Leave Laura alone, there's a good chap", and he'd take some notice of you?'

'No, but – but I do know one or two things about him, so he'd have to be a bit careful.'

'And you wouldn't be in the least bit scared of being done over by a couple of his criminal friends one dark night after school – which is what'd happen to you if you tried *that* one?'

'Maybe I could –'

'Or your dad attacked one day when he's out alone on the estate.'

'He's tough, he is.'

'As tough as two toughs?'

But through all this talking, Jake was beginning to get more of a grip on himself. He suddenly cut me short with, 'Yeah, but all this is supposing that you tell on me or I tell on you, and I'm not going to. Are you?'

'I might,' I said coldly. 'Apart from being afraid of getting beaten up, give me one good reason why I shouldn't.'

'Getting beaten up *is* the good reason.'

'You said you wouldn't let that happen.'

'I might, if you told.'

'But would you?'

He gave me a flash of his dark eyes and an unpleasant smile that told me it was going to be even more difficult than I'd thought, then said, 'It's better for me if you don't know whether I would or wouldn't, isn't it?'

There was no getting any further with that line of attack. It was time to change.

'Anyway, you still haven't answered my question. Why are you doing Steve Mallinson's dirty work for him?'

It was no good, I was pushing too hard. Jake only muttered, 'Because he asked me to,' then stood up, looking over me to the doorway.

'Have you been out there?' he asked.

'Not right out. I've crawled to with my head out and my hands on the platform – and Robyn holding on to my ankle.'

'I bet I'd dare.'

'You probably would.'

'I'm gonna try. Now.'

'Why?'

'Well, because . . .'

'So you could show off to me?'

'No, but –'

'So you could show me what a big brave boy you are, and "Gosh, I'm mates with Steve Mallinson too"?'

'Mind out of the way.'

He pushed roughly past me, up and on to the flat bit, then stopped, putting his hands out to hold on to each side of the doorway. For some reason, I suddenly felt absolutely positive that the one thing I'd got to do was to stop him going out there. If I could only do that, I'd win him over.

His knuckles were white. He wasn't just holding the sides of the doorway, he was gripping tight.

'It's quite wide, really, the platform,' he said.

I knew he was lying. That is just not the thing that strikes you when you first see it from up here.

'And you say it's strong enough for one person?' he asked.

'That was only a story.'

'What? It didn't really happen?'

'I don't know.'

'And all that about the Roman guards and that. Was that not true either?'

'Maybe not. I don't know. Maybe they were Norman.'

'My dad says this thing's called the Obelisk not the Ziggurat, and it's not that old.'

'It's called the Ziggurat as far as anyone I trust is concerned, and it is that old.' Yet at the same time as I felt myself struggling to keep his belief in my Ziggurat, I knew he'd handed me the key. After a moment I said, 'Your dad's going to be a very lonely person if you get killed daring yourself to go out there.'

There was an even longer pause while he stood there, gripping, looking out. The wind gave a couple of extra hard gusts, buffeting the Ziggurat as if to say it was coming to help me this time.

Sure enough, the next thing he said was, 'Yow, it's fantastically windy out there. Maybe I'd better wait till it calms down a bit.'

He turned round very gingerly, reaching out for something to hold on to, as if suddenly frightened that he was going to be sucked out through the doorway. He came to the top stair and stood looking down at me.

It was time to take the risk. Either he'd tell me to get lost or he'd start to be won over, but there was never going to be a better time than this.

'Jake, we need your help against Steve,' I said.

'Me? Why me?' he was surprised, but not shocked or angry.

'Because you're the only one that can. I *know*.'

He stared at me for a long time, then said, 'Who's "we"?'

'Oh, me, Robyn, everyone in our year – just about everyone in the school. Even you. He's got to be stopped.'

'Why?'

'You know why. Because what he does is wrong. Because he makes everyone behave wrongly. Because he's vile and horrible.'

'But why me? What can I do?'

I bit back the word 'magic', but if anyone had it, it was Jake now, with the arch of the doorway and the sky behind him.

'I don't know exactly,' I said. 'I just know you can. You're the only one that's strong enough.'

I knew at last that he wanted to believe me. It was just

that he couldn't quite – yet. To stop him from beginning to talk himself out of it, I got up without another word and started off down the stairs. A few seconds later I heard him following.

Robyn : The Katy Marsh Incident

Well, Laura had said I was OK unless something happened, but it did – the very next Monday. It wasn't anything to do with my letter to the *Chronicle*.

There was a girl in my tutor group called Katy Marsh who was quite a good friend. When I'd first gone round trying to get some support together for not giving in to Steve, she'd been the first to agree. In fact she'd also been one of the few who'd managed to avoid buying a book, not only this term but the term before as well.

She managed it by making herself appear even more scatterbrained than she really was. She'd been challenged to produce her book twice last half term – once by Gary Talbot and once by Mike Telford, another fourth-former who did heavy work for Steve – but she'd pretended she'd left it in the cloakroom, then forgotten to turn up with it, saying that one of them had told her one thing, and another something else, and so on. She just kept putting them off and going all silly when they tried to pin her down. You know – saying things like, 'I'm *sure* I had it with me', and 'You'll never believe how stupid I am'.

Anyway, it turned out that they'd caught up with her after school on Friday, just as she was going out of the gate. Steve Mallinson, Martin Dwyer, Gary Talbot *and* Mike Telford had all been there in a bunch, so she'd had no chance of playing one off against the other the way she usually did.

You've no idea how innocent those people can make it all look, by the way. They lean against the wall of the school grounds, lazily shouting greetings to their mates as they come out. Then when their victim appears one of them saunters over to collect him or her, as if there was nothing important about it at all, and brings them over to the group. Any teacher coming past only sees a first-year standing chatting with a bunch of fourth-years and probably thinks how nice it is. 'How well the different age groups mix in our school!'

They'd made Katy get her purse out, and it happened she had a five-pound note in it because it was her mother's birthday at the weekend, and she'd been going to buy her a really decent present on the way home. They do that sort of thing a lot in Katy's family.

Instead of charging Katy the money she was supposed to 'owe' them, Martin Dwyer had pocketed the whole fiver, saying it was because she was a trouble-maker. And when she'd made a fuss there'd been the usual threats, of course. So she'd had to go home and pretend she'd lost the money.

Apart from the injustice of the whole thing, what completely made my blood boil was the fact that Katy's family is not at all well off. Her dad's an invalid, and it's her mother who goes out to work in a petrol station to keep him and Katy and her sister, as well as looking after the house. That was another reason Katy wanted to get her a nice present – to say 'thank you'.

When Katy told me all this, just before the tutor group period we always have on Mondays, I knew Laura had been wrong to tell me to wait. Something had to be done there and then. I was going to get that

86

money back for Katy, and since it certainly wasn't worth asking anyone to help me, I'd got to do it alone.

One period of maths and one of English did nothing to cool me down. In fact the anger kept bursting up inside, so that I found it impossible to concentrate and got told off a couple of times, which is unusual for me.

I had no clear plan as I marched across the playground to Steve's office that break – my own little army of me alone – but I had ideas jigging around in my brain in time with my footsteps.

I'm going straight to the Head. He's already prepared to listen.

If he won't listen, I'm going to the police.

I've written a letter, and if anything happens to me they'll find it.

I was so sure of myself that when I suddenly saw Steve out in the playground, leaning against a wall with Martin Dwyer and a couple of girl hangers-on round him, I was filled with joy. I went straight up so quickly that I was standing in front of him almost before he'd noticed me arrive.

'Steve Mallinson!' I shrieked at his face. 'You're going to give Katy Marsh her five pounds back, or I'm going directly to the police.'

He reacted with amazing speed considering what a surprise it must have been. He levered himself off the wall, gave the briefest of glances around over my head, then brought his hand back and slapped my cheek, very hard. It still tingles when I think about it, but at the time it wasn't pain that got me – just the incredible shock. It took my breath away, prevented me from saying another word.

As I stood there gasping, tears coming to my eyes, he

bent down and hissed, 'Stay there if you want another of those. If not, get away – smart.'

One of the girls behind me giggled nervously. I stood it for another second or two, then couldn't control my hands going up to protect my face. I knew it meant I was beaten. I turned and walked back the way I'd come, completely broken. The best that can be said for me is that I didn't actually burst into sobs till I was out of his sight.

I managed to get to the toilets without being seen and hide there for the rest of break, sneaking out to the basins to dab cold water on my bright red cheek and inspect my face for blotchiness when there was no one in. I knew I didn't want to tell anybody what had happened, maybe not even Laura. I was too ashamed at how easily I'd crumbled.

It was easy for other people months later to tell me what I should have done. They said I should have gone straight to a teacher with my cheek still red, and reported Steve. He would have denied it, of course, but almost certainly those girls who'd been there would not have been able to keep lying if someone had questioned them hard. What's more, Steve wouldn't have dared to have me 'done' out of school if there'd been a really thorough investigation of his setup going on.

But you can see those kinds of things afterwards. At the time I'd have had to believe that one of the teachers would take it seriously enough to start investigating at once, that they'd do it properly enough to get at the truth, and that they'd be able to see I was protected – and that's a lot to expect of one person. You could trust the nice teachers to take it seriously and the hard teachers to do it properly, but there didn't seem to be one you could trust to do both.

In fact it was always, always the same problem: if you took the first step and it failed, you'd be completely exposed. That was why none of us dared to take the first step.

Anyway, that was on the Monday. On the Tuesday morning, Gary Talbot stopped me in the corridor and told me Steve wanted to see me that dinnertime.

Even though I'd been half expecting it, I went into a flat panic. I had absolutely no idea what to do. Steve had cautioned me last time, so he wasn't just going to say the same thing again. He was either going to hit me again himself, or he was going to tell me I'd be 'done'.

Gradually I found myself almost wanting dinnertime to come because I simply couldn't stand any more waiting around not knowing what was going to happen to me. As I didn't live in Ashleigh itself, I felt I might be reasonably safe from his outside thugs going to and from school, but then I pictured them suddenly turning up in Pikestone village. Or might I find them on the bus home one night, or might they even go for my parents in some way? Or perhaps I'd just be endlessly got at in school in ways I couldn't even begin to imagine yet, but which they'd take a lot of pleasure in dreaming up.

The possibilities twisted this way and that, till in the end I simply had to get some advice from Laura in morning break. It meant telling her the whole story, and, as I expected, she called me a fool for getting in even deeper when the one thing I'd been supposed to do was keep quiet.

'I was beginning to get things moving,' she said furiously. 'Because if we rush it, the magic will all go sour on us, and –'

'Will you stop talking about magic,' I screamed back

at her. 'This is for real, Laura. What am I actually going to do? I've got an hour and a half to decide.'

'Don't go,' she said.

'Don't go?'

'No. It might give us that bit more time. Don't go, and then make sure you're never, never alone. Keep together with a bunch of us, all the time.'

'There aren't a bunch of us in Pikestone.'

'I don't think they'll try Pikestone – not for a while, anyway. They'll try to get you here first.'

I took her advice. She was the only friend I had that I could really trust, so I'd have been stupid not to. I kept with gangs of first-years all dinner hour and hid my face every time I saw a fourth-year.

Just as we were all going in for afternoon school I saw Martin Dwyer and Mike Telford pushing their way through my classmates towards me. There was no chance at all that anyone would risk trying to stop them if they started to get nasty, though I felt pretty sure they wouldn't dare – not so near the main entrance.

And that gave me a bright idea. The teacher on dinner-break duty was standing by the door, keeping order as people went through. I skirted round the side of the crowd so that I was able to come up behind him.

'Excuse me,' I said, then – the first thing I could think of, because I didn't know him at all – 'Are you taking us for English this afternoon?'

He turned round and said, 'Why?' with great surprise.

'Oh, er, somebody told me you were.'

'I very much doubt it,' he said, nearly laughing. 'For one thing I've got a full teaching programme this afternoon; for another, I don't teach the first two years at all; and for yet another I usually don't teach English – just boring old physics.'

'Oh, sorry,' I said. 'It must have been someone else.'

'My pleasure,' he said, still smiling at me.

In spite of all that smiling, which would have told anyone I wasn't reporting anything serious, it had done the trick. I could see the backs of those two thugs disappearing, going in the opposite direction to the crowd.

Jake : Changing Faces

When I left Laura by the Ziggurat (or whatever she wanted to call it) that Sunday afternoon, I was feeling pretty fed up. Why is it, I was thinking as I jogged home along the downhill path, that every time you seem to be on to something good, someone – usually an adult – has to come along and say, 'No, that's dangerous', or 'No, that's wrong'?

This time it hadn't been an adult but another kid, and she'd said both to me. She'd stopped me testing myself on that platform and she'd tried to tell me I ought to start going against the one person who'd been really decent to me since I'd arrived here. And all because *she* thought I might kill myself and Dad would be lonely; *she* thought Steve was bad.

In fact – and I hadn't mentioned this to her – Steve was being particularly good to me just then. He'd had a quick word with me at break on Friday, and he'd said that as I was behaving like a big lad, I might like to learn what it was to be a big lad. He and his mates were going to this Mike Telford's house to watch a video straight after school on Monday, and it was 'a real grown-up video' and I could come along if I wanted. I wasn't, of course, to tell anyone.

'And I hope you've got a strong stomach, young Jake lad,' he'd said. 'Because this one is strictly adults only.'

Martin Dwyer went sniggering on to himself for

ages after he'd said that, but I couldn't see why. I'd seen a few horror films and I didn't reckon I was afraid of anything on a video.

All I'd got to do now was square it with Dad, because I'd be late back so I'd have to take my bike – there was no bus out to Pikestone after the school one. I thought it was probably better not to tell him I was actually going to see a video, because he was bound to start asking questions about who with and what video.

So when I got back from the Ziggurat I told Dad I'd be staying late the next day to go to a meeting of the school Geography Society, just to see what it was like. You see, I thought that after I'd seen the video, I could tell him I'd decided to do that instead – and it would be too late for him to say no.

It was embarrassing then, because he started getting all keen on me joining the Geography Society. He said it was the first evidence I'd shown of being interested in anything other than booting at footballs or falling out of trees with my monkey mates (he'd always called that gang I used to have at the other place my 'monkey mates'). To steer him away from the subject, I suddenly asked him on the spur of the moment what he thought about bullying. I don't know what put that idea into my head – just that anything seemed better than him going on about the Geography Society.

He answered with a bit of poetry, the way he occasionally does when something sparks him off. He's been reading quite a lot since Mum went.

'Oh, it is excellent
To have a giant's strength: but it is tyrannous
To use it like a giant.'

Then he said, 'Shakespeare – just about says it all,

really, doesn't it? Why, is someone bullying you at school?'

'No. No.'

'Or are you bullying someone?'

I had a flash of a picture of myself with Philip Crowther. That wasn't really bullying, was it? I mean, I hadn't actually done anything to him. But the thought must have made me hesitate a second, because Dad followed up with, 'You're very big for your age, you know.'

'No,' I said quickly. 'Nothing like that.'

'Then why do you ask?'

Having got myself into the mess, I had to give some reason. 'Oh, well, it's just that I think there might be some bullying going on in the school. I don't know who.'

He looked at me for a long, long time. He's got very piercing eyes when he stares at you. Then he said quietly, 'If you ever find out who, you must fight him with all your strength and courage, and even cunning. There! That's what I think about bullying. It's the lowest of the low.'

'Yeah,' I said. 'I don't think there's anything much really.'

In fact I did worry quite a bit about what Dad had said – well, it wasn't even so much what he said, which I'd mostly heard before from my old head teacher, as the powerful way he said it. Almost as if it was one of the things that mattered most to him in the whole world.

It didn't have anything to do with watching a video, though – at least, not as far as I could see – so next day when Mike Telford gave me a slip of paper with an address on it, I went straight there the moment school was over.

The place was a fairly ordinary semi in a row of others like it – not too difficult to find, though I needed to ask a couple of times. Having my bike with me, I was way ahead of the others and had to hang about outside till they came – Steve, Martin and Mike, but not Gary.

When he saw me, Steve said, 'Well, well. Here's the Jake person with his tongue hanging out for a bit of blood,' and Martin did quite a lot more of his evil laughing. Meanwhile Mike was letting us in with his key.

When we went into the living room, which again was ordinary and neat, the three of them immediately crowded round together in front of the video, shuffling boxes and whispering and giggling, leaving me standing at the back. When they'd finally chosen one and slotted it in, Steve pointed me to the best armchair of all, right out in front, nearest the telly. Then they sat down around and a bit behind me, and the film began.

'You'll enjoy this one, Jake lad,' Steve's voice came, as the creepy music started and the titles rolled up over a hideous face changing into even more hideous shapes. 'It's got some really good bits in it.'

'Yeah – bits of people,' said Mike.

'I was gonna say that,' Martin complained.

'Yeah, well you need your head sharpened.'

'Put 'im in the head sharpener!'

I don't know if you've ever seen one of those kinds of video. This one's called 'Plasmic Surgery', and it begins with this man lying on his bed, then he starts going red in the face, then purple, then black. He starts clawing at the neck of his shirt to get it open, moaning and screaming all the time, then suddenly his whole head opens up in a slow sort of explosion. They'd made it seem even more real by gradually blocking out the picture with red and grey blotches, and plops and slaps on the soundtrack, as if bits of him were actually slamming into the camera lens.

The one thing you can say for those videos is that they are certainly not boring. I was on the edge of my seat from the very beginning, till suddenly I found it was getting to me as I started to follow the story. Apparently all that first bit had just been in the imagination of this person who was completely round the twist. The trouble was that the more things like that he kept imagining about people's faces (and there were some, I can tell you!) the madder he thought he was getting, till he started to try and make things like that really happen, so as to prove to himself he wasn't mad.

It sounds corny when you tell the story like that, but all the gruesome bits are so real that they do get to you. I began frantically telling myself that it was all just tomato ketchup and bits of meat or plastic, and tricks like that, but it went on and on. I began to long for those normal bits in between the horrors where ordinary people just talked – except that I knew it was all going to explode into another horror any moment.

I was so deep in it, out there alone at the front, that for a long time I didn't notice the mutters and little snorts of laughter going on behind me – until I had to shut my eyes at one scene I could tell was going to be especially disgusting. Then I heard their whispers.

'He's got his eyes shut.'

(Giggles.)

'Shall we wake him up? He's missing the best bits – that eyeball there.'

(Giggles.)

'Naw, it must be nearly his bedtime.'

It wasn't at all what they'd intended, but I think maybe that was the only thing that saved me from being sick or having to get up and go out (if I'd have dared). I didn't say or do anything to show I knew, but it cut me off from the film, which became less real than what was going on in the room.

I began instead to think about what they were doing. I wasn't being included with the big lads at all. They'd sat me out here in front so that they could watch me watching a video they'd probably seen a dozen times themselves. They hoped I was going to wet myself or do something ridiculous, either just for their own fun or because then they'd have even more power over me – or both.

Well, it wasn't going to be like that. I got a grip and began concentrating really hard, pretending to be all involved in what was happening on the screen. What I concentrated on in fact was a small picture of a country cottage on the wall just above the telly. And every time I couldn't help my eyes being dragged down to some piece of vileness on the screen I repeated, 'Ketchup and plastic; ketchup and plastic . . .' over and over to myself. Then I even managed to crown it by looking round and smiling at one of them every time something happened that I knew was supposed to be making me sick, as if I was having a really great time.

It began to work. The giggling died down; the whispering changed. They were starting to talk about other things than me or the video. They were obviously getting bored with the whole experiment.

I was saved from having to keep up the act much longer by the sound of the front door opening. Well, it wasn't so much that I understood what the sound was myself as that Mike suddenly scrambled to his feet, saying, 'Christ! Mum's knocked off early.'

He dashed over to get the remote they'd left lying on the video, and next moment 'Plasmic Surgery' had been replaced by 'Neighbours', which luckily happened to be on by then, just as the living-room door opened. I was so coolly in control by that stage that I couldn't help laughing to myself at the idea of how great it would have been if instead of switching to 'Neighbours', the telly had come up with 'Bodger and Badger, and Mike's mum had come in and found us all apparently watching that.

Steve was also cool – but then he usually was – giving her one of his dazzling smiles and saying, 'Hope you don't mind us being here, Mrs Telford. Just came in to catch "Neighbours".'

She looked round the room at us unsmiling, without coming fully in, then said, 'All right, as long as you don't leave a mess,' and backed out again.

So we watched our way through to the end of 'Neighbours', then went home. The only thing that was said outside was when Steve asked me, 'Enjoy it?'

'I'll say!' I said enthusiastically. 'It was great.'

He just answered, 'Mm, pity you couldn't see to the end,' as if he was still hoping that *that* part at least would have made me sick.

Big boys! I thought, as I cycled back home. Big boys! That brief sight of them all in front of Mrs Telford had cut them more down to size than I'd have thought possible. Just the same as little kids caught with their hands in the sugar bowl, really.

How I'd have reacted if the whole thing had gone according to *their* plan, I can't say. I'd probably have got home still feeling shaken, and muttered a few more lies about the Geography Society to Dad.

As it was, I went in to find him getting the tea things out on the table and I said straight away, 'I'm sorry, Dad. I didn't get to the Geography Society after all. One of the lads had a video we wanted to see, so we went back to his house instead.'

'Oh,' he said, trying to look interested rather than disappointed. Then he shot me one of his searching looks. 'Nasty one, was it?'

'Erm. . . . Yeah, well it was, actually.'

'And did you enjoy it?'

'No,' I said. 'It was complete and utter rubbish. Just ketchup and plastic.'

The fact that I suddenly deeply felt that as I said it must have come across to him, because he paused, stooping to get the potatoes out of the oven, and smiled up at me.

'Well,' he said, 'perhaps you've learned something a lot more valuable than you'd have got from the Geography Society, then.'

'I might go to that next week,' I said, wanting to please him.

'I'll believe it when you tell me you've been,' he said – but quite pleasantly.

On Wednesday Gary Talbot told me that Steve wanted to see me in the office. I slipped in as usual to find just him and Martin there.

'You know that girl Robyn in your year, don't you?' said Steve at once. 'In fact she lives near you, doesn't she?'

'Yes,' I said doubtfully, not knowing what was coming.

'Well, I want her hassled.'

'Hassled? How . . .?'

'I want her hassled as much and as hard as you can possibly do it.' It was more than firm – almost angry – the way he was speaking. 'And what's more, you're to report to me what you've done – here, every day. I want her life made a bleeding misery.'

'Why, what's she done?'

'Never mind what she's done. That's my business. Yours is just to hassle her.'

'But I don't understand what I've got to do.'

Martin Dwyer was keen to explain. 'There's lots of ways. You make it look like accidents. Knock her school bag or something out of her hand where it's muddy, then go to get it for her but tip it out instead. Then tread on the things, trying to help her pick them up.'

'Just kick her ankles as you go past,' said Steve. 'Every time. Spit in her face.'

'She'd know that wasn't an accident. She'd report me.'

'Not if she knows I'm behind it.'

'But that's just it. She doesn't.'

'Well, tell her, then, if you're too scared to do it off your own bat.'

'But – but I thought the idea was that no one was supposed to know that I –'

'Listen!' Steve put his face right close to mine. The veins on his forehead were standing out like little snakes, his eyes were sharp with fury. 'I want that girl hassled. And you're gonna do it. Understood?'

I nodded. There wasn't much else to do, but my own anger was beginning to grow now. I left him there quickly, before I said something stupid, and went straight to find Laura.

100

She was in the middle of a group of her friends. Without explaining, I beckoned her out of it and she came at once.

'Laura,' I said quietly, 'I'm going to help you against Steve Mallinson. Tell Robyn, but only Robyn.'

Laura :
Cunning Against Magic?

It was definitely a case for the Ziggurat. As I've said, getting up there on weekdays wasn't so easy because our parents weren't too happy about me and Robyn going out after tea unless they knew we were at each other's houses.

Then I had the bright idea of arranging a picnic for Thursday. The June weather had settled down into a fine period, so it seemed quite a reasonable thing to do – Robyn and I had done similar things the summer before. As soon as we got back from school, we'd make sandwiches and so on, then go out, and we could be home again almost before our parents had finished tea.

There was one problem, though, as Jake pointed out when I suggested it on the bus home that Wednesday. He told us what Steve expected him to do to Robyn, then said, 'The trouble is, I'm going to have to go to him tomorrow and say I did something this evening or tomorrow morning. If I don't he'll only get someone else on to it *and* be after me too.'

Robyn hadn't said much. She'd been pale-looking and fairly silent ever since the Monday, when Steve had hit her. Now all she did was to say unhappily, 'I'm being a problem to you, and it's all my fault. You'd better let them get on with it.'

I'd almost run out of things to cheer her up with by

102

then, and couldn't manage more than, 'Hey, come on. It's not that bad.'

It was Jake who got a spark out of her. His eyes lit up as if she'd given him a challenge he was really going to enjoy.

'No, it'll be great!' he said suddenly. 'All we've got to do is invent something I've done to you that'll show, and then you've got to act as if I'd done it.'

'But what?' Robyn asked. The good thing was, though, that she wasn't asking it in a hopeless sort of way. You could see her mind beginning to work again.

'Couldn't we actually do something right in front of him or one of his gang?' said Jake. 'Something we have ready, but we don't do it till we see them looking.'

'Like you kicking Robyn, you mean?'

'No. Too difficult to make it look right – not without actually hurting her, anyway.'

'You'll just have to hurt me, then,' Robyn said miserably. 'It's better than one of them doing it.'

We all sat silent and gloomy for a minute or two then, racking our brains while the bus rattled on towards Pikestone. There wasn't a lot of time left to decide.

'I know!' Robyn said suddenly. 'We could break something of mine – something that's already broken, but we just fix up a bit, then let it go. Jake'd only have to be near me for it to look good. I could do the rest.'

'What about your school bag?'

She pulled a face. 'It may be old, but it's not broken yet.'

'Well what else?'

'I know!' she said again. 'I've got an old Walkman that doesn't work any more –'

'But we're not allowed those in school.'

'Even better. If a teacher sees it fall on the floor, I'll

103

get into trouble for having it, so it'll seem even nastier.' She must have noticed our anxious expressions, because she added, 'Don't worry, I won't get into *much* trouble – not with my beautiful reputation. I'll just say I'd brought it in to get it mended in town. They can't get me for using it when it doesn't even work.'

It was wonderful to see the old fire back in her. It was wonderful to have Jake with us. In spite of his dealings with Steve, both Robyn and I trusted him completely and at once. It wasn't because of the magic in him – I knew he had that, but magic can be bad or good, cunning or honest. I can't say it better than I did in my thoughtbook – I must have written it that evening:

If Steve is a black wizard, Jake is a blind wizard.
 The Blind Wizard goes straight because he cannot see the twists and turns of the path. His power is the strength of straightness.
 Because he cannot see, he follows straight to the call of the strongest voice.
 The True Voice of the Ziggurat grows stronger than the voice of the Black Wizard!!

Actually, our picnic at the Ziggurat next day, which was to have been a serious, sober planning meeting, began as a great giggle. Robyn's idea had worked brilliantly . . .

[Jake : What Robyn and I did was, when we came in through the main gate in the morning, we went on and round the block and out through the side gate, then in at the front gate again, with me walking a little way behind Robyn. We did this three times, till at last we found ourselves going in through the main gate just behind Gary Talbot. Then I accelerated so as to pass Robyn, giving her just a bit of a nudge, and she dropped the Walkman on the ground.

She'd prepared it fantastically well. It fell into about a hundred pieces all over the place, and at the same time she let out a great, 'Oh, NO!!'

Of course I'd walked on – not only past her but past Gary Talbot too – so it would seem as if I was trying not to be connected with what had happened. When she did that yell, though, I was able to stop and look round quite naturally. Gary and his friends were standing there gazing back at all these pieces, while Robyn was on her hands and knees on the ground, apparently trying to get them together in a panic and failing miserably because more people kept coming in and treading them even further to pieces.

The best thing was when Gary began to stare around, a bit puzzled. He saw me looking back, and I grinned and gave him a huge wink. He gave me a knowing little nod and thumbs-up to show me that he was clever enough to understand exactly what had gone on – except that he wasn't, and didn't.

He'd already told Steve about it when I reported at dinnertime. Steve was still thrilled to bits. He kept punching his fist into his palm and saying, 'That's the way, Jake lad! Keep at her till she comes crawling.']

. . . That was why, when we arrived at the Ziggurat, Jake and Robyn spent a long time doing all that 'Wasn't it great when . . .?' and 'Did you see his face?' and 'You should have been there!' that they'd already done a lot of on the bus home.

You must understand what it was like for us – for Robyn especially. She'd spent much of the year hating

Steve, the last few weeks in terror of him, but now, for the first time ever, she was beginning to believe that he might not always have things exactly his own way.

When they'd calmed down a bit, we decided on a good dry patch of tufty grass and ate our sandwiches there – even though it was over an hour earlier than we'd have been having tea at home. We ate outside in the sun, hardly talking at all, and it was so quiet and peaceful in the clearing that it was almost impossible to believe in those threats and dangers only a few miles off. I kept looking up at the Ziggurat, wondering what level of discussion this was going to be. In one sense it was of course top-level, but I had this very, very strong feeling that we were going to have to reserve the top level for something even more important.

I ended up suggesting that we shouldn't go into the Ziggurat at all just yet. I thought Jake looked a little relieved, as if he'd been feeling he might have to dare himself again to go out on the platform if we did go up to the top. Robyn just nodded. I knew quite well that she didn't really think the Ziggurat mattered one way or another, except to please me.

Then I said what had been on my mind since Jake had told me he'd help us and the dream of resisting Steve had begun to seem as if it could possibly come true someday.

'This business of fooling Steve Mallinson about what Jake's supposed to be doing to Robyn – I mean, it's good, but it isn't anything really. It isn't getting at him at all, it's only protecting Robyn, and only a bit, and only till he finds out, which he's more likely to do the longer we go on trying it. I mean, we're going to run out of tricks soon, aren't we?'

'But we've only just started,' Jake complained.

'Yes,' said Robyn. 'We've got to begin in a small way, and build up from there – get more and more people on our side.'

I had a job to keep my patience with them. 'But don't you see? You can't get people on your side that way. Who'd be interested, and who are you going to tell, anyway? The moment you tell any single person except us here, the whole trick's blown open and Steve can move in and get us one by one, or even all three of us together.'

'OK then,' said Robyn. 'We can try and get support but still keep that a secret.'

'Which is exactly what you were trying to do before. And look what happened.'

There was a long silence. Only the birds in the trees around us made any sound.

Jake looked sideways at me. 'What do *you* suggest, then?'

'We've got to get to the heart of it. Steve himself. Those others would be nothing but cheap little bullies without Steve's magic. He holds them together. They – we – everyone – we're all under his spell.'

'Please stop talking magic, Laura,' said Robyn tiredly. 'It doesn't help when we're trying to sort out an actual urgent problem.'

'That *is* the actual problem!' I shouted back at her. 'OK!' I was near screaming with impatience. 'Let me put it in very little baby words for you then, Robyn Somers. The problem you won't face up to is this: *people like him!* That's why no one's going to get up and go round waving flags and shouting 'Down with Steve Mallinson'. They like him. They love him. That's what being under his spell means, if that's the only way you can understand it.'

'They don't like him,' said Robyn, but she didn't sound absolutely sure. '*I* don't.'

'Well, that's why you're alone, isn't it? You're different.'

'You mean, people actually like forking out 30p for those tatty little books?'

'In a way, yes! They aren't just books, they're like badges. They show you belong.'

'And they like buying bike insurance?'

'They don't have to unless they're stupid or difficult – or different. Anyway, that's another thing. When was the last time anybody had a bike damaged at school and it wasn't done on purpose by Martin Dwyer?'

'I dunno.'

'But at other schools it happens all the time. Doesn't it, Jake?'

'I suppose it does. Certainly did at my last school even though we didn't have any bullying there. Things got nicked off 'em, mainly.'

'Yes, but they don't at Ashleigh High. So Steve actually keeps bikes safe for people. If he's there, there can't be anything worse. Even those thugs of his would probably go round beating up more people than they actually do, if he didn't hold power over them. *Now* do you understand?'

'Well, I understand what you're saying,' said Robyn. She got up and started to walk around. 'But I'm not sure it's true, and I don't see what it's got to do with magic, really, and I don't see how it helps us decide what to do. As far as I can see, it just makes everything seem even more hopeless – as if it's not worth trying to do anything against Steve because there'd only be something worse instead.'

For a while I couldn't answer her because I'd never

before actually worked things out in the way I'd just put them to her. The thought of all those courtiers and cooks in the story of Sleeping Beauty came into my mind suddenly – all lying happily in their deep hundred-year sleep. Had the Prince really been a villain to come bursting through the hedge of thorns, breaking the spell and waking them all up?

In the end I said, 'Yes, we do have to fight Steve, because he's evil, and if worse comes after him we'll have to fight that too. And no, it's not hopeless, but we've got to get to the heart of it. We have to know more about Steve. We've got to find out about him and his weak spots.'

'Huh! Fat chance of that, when we can't even get near him – except to get threatened or hit. And I'm not choosing to do *that* again.'

'I can,' said Jake. 'Get near him, I mean. I do, every day.'

'Then that could be it!' I got up and began to walk around too.

'What could be what?' Jake asked. 'What am I supposed to find out?'

'His weak spots – like I said.'

'He hasn't got any. He isn't a coward, he isn't stupid by a long way, he's strong –'

'He must have a weakness. Everyone's got at least one.'

Jake had got up too by now, so that we were all wandering round in different directions, half shouting things to each other. Robyn had gone some way off, though evidently she could still hear what Jake and I were saying. 'He gets angry,' she called to us across the clearing.

'Everyone gets angry,' I shouted back.

'Not as much as he does. He goes raging mad if anyone laughs at him – or challenges him.'

'So?'

'It's a weakness, I think. Though it doesn't feel like a weakness when you're on the receiving end.'

'She's right,' said Jake. 'He does get angry, but I don't know what good that is to us.'

'There may be other things . . .' I said half-heartedly, not caring much if anyone heard me or not because it was a fairly useless thing to say. The truth was that it was me who was near to losing heart now.

'Anyway,' Jake said, 'whatever else we decide, we've got to find something for me to say I've done to Robyn tomorrow. Then we've at least got the weekend to think about things.'

Anything seemed better than carrying on wandering about the way we were doing.

'OK,' I shouted. 'Let's go in the Ziggurat and decide. Level two.'

'What d'you mean, level two?'

I'd forgotten that Jake didn't know about my levels. I'd got used to Robyn going along with me but not really caring. Now I half expected him to laugh when I explained about the different levels for different kinds of problem.

But he didn't laugh. Instead he said, 'Why not top level now? It is pretty important, isn't it? Or maybe couldn't this be that special kind of problem you say the fourth level's waiting for?'

'No, we're not going anywhere near the top because you'll only start worrying about how you ought to dare yourself to go out on the platform, and we've got more urgent things to do.'

110

'I think I've got to try it soon, though,' he said thoughtfully.

'That's your problem, then.' I shrugged impatiently. I really couldn't see that it mattered to anyone, him testing his courage on the Ziggurat as if it was some kind of fairground ride. I decided we'd be better off not going in at all until we were ready to discuss the whole thing more seriously.

Jake : Failure

It would have been difficult to find any idea for fooling Steve to equal what Robyn and I had done that morning. In the end, remembering that Philip Crowther incident, I suggested the easiest thing might be just to hand her pencil case over to him as if I'd nicked it. She wasn't too keen on that at first, of course, because she'd just had a new one for her birthday, till Laura pointed out that it needn't be that one. We could find any old pencil case, and all chip in with things to fill it.

So that's what we did. Next morning Laura brought along an old one of hers that she'd managed to scrub her name off and write Robyn's on instead. Then on the bus going in we all contributed bits from our own – pens, felt pens, pencils, crayons and all that sort of stuff.

I took it to the office at break. Martin Dwyer and Mike Telford were there as well. As I'd feared, Steve wasn't too thrilled this time. He opened it and gave a disgusted sort of sniff.

'I should think she'd be glad to lose this,' he said. 'And anyway, does she know it's been nicked?'

'She probably thinks she chucked it in the bin,' said Martin, looking over Steve's shoulder. 'Why don't you get the lads on to her?'

'Because we don't wanna use them too often,' Steve said. 'Anyway, it costs us. And because we want that

112

Robyn bitch to come to her senses. Chances are, if we just got her done over she'd start whining to everybody.'

'So? We'd be in the clear, wouldn't we?'

'Steve would, you mean,' said Mike Telford.

I pricked up my ears at that. It was the very first time I'd heard any of them dare to suggest that there could be anything wrong in Steve's setup. For a second I had a wild little hope that things could be falling apart for some reason I didn't know about. Steve quickly killed that one, though.

'Mike,' was all he said – very quietly, almost as if he was only announcing the person who was going to speak next.

And sure enough, Mike did. 'Yeah, I meant that Steve would too.'

'You're gonna have to do better than this, Jake lad,' said Steve, handing the pencil case back to me. 'Trouble is, you're trying to keep your nose too clean.'

For very different reasons from Steve, I couldn't help agreeing with both those statements.

The three of us met by the Ziggurat twice that weekend, but we simply couldn't seem to get any further. Robyn thought she had a great idea when she suggested writing down everything we knew about Steve, then making hundreds of copies of it and showering them everywhere.

Laura and I both jumped on that one and squashed it flat. Laura said if we didn't put our names on it, who'd take it seriously? In any case, Steve would suspect Robyn first, and see no harm in getting at her for it. And if we did put our names on it and she was right about people liking Steve, they'd only hate us for telling tales and trying to bring him down. Probably, after Steve had played the hurt innocent for a bit, we'd be accused of lying out of spite or something.

I pointed out that making hundreds of copies of anything at 10p a copy would cost us a bomb, and as far as I knew we none of us had that sort of money.

Next Robyn started on about getting parents and teachers to help. The trouble was that even after we'd whittled the list of teachers down to those we could actually talk to and who might try and do something (and that wasn't many, I can tell you), there was still the fact that we had absolutely no real evidence; so it was again going to look like tale-telling, especially if nothing against Steve was found.

As for parents, we all had different reasons for not wanting to involve our own, and it obviously wasn't a lot of use trying to involve anybody else's! Robyn was anxious about her mum's health, what with her expecting, and she felt she'd more or less promised not to worry her dad – even if he'd have been any good anyway. I wasn't going to tell my dad, because I felt he'd despise me for doing so instead of coping with the problem myself. Laura refused as well. She said her mum and dad were worriers too, and they wouldn't know what to do in any case, because she wasn't in direct danger herself.

Robyn had to agree finally, though she said she was still certain that the only thing to do was to get someone organized somehow. Laura still kept on about the need to 'break Steve's spell'.

As for me, all I could suggest was that we'd got to deal with the problem facing us now – thinking up some more tricks for the following week. And that in the end was what we spent most of our time doing.

Not actually harming Robyn was still the main difficulty, but what was extra hard was trying to make it believable that she didn't know it was me doing it. None of us wanted me to be exposed as working for Steve just when we were hoping to get more people on our side – even Laura had to agree that we'd need that eventually. Put those together with trying to make it all look convincing to Steve, and you'll see we had our work cut out.

Anyway, although we had a lot of fun trying to think up ideas that grew wilder and wilder, this was the best we could actually come up with for real. This was our final 'list':

On Monday Robyn was going to wear an old skirt and blouse, and come out of school in the middle of a crowd of people including me. I was going to pretend to trip her from behind and she was going to fall – if possible into a puddle but, if it was dry, on to the hard muddy patch under the conker trees. Then she'd accuse someone else, not me, of tripping her, while I'd go on past Steve's mob at the gate and wink at them.

On Tuesday she would have to trade on her good reputation with the teachers and show them her maths homework all torn up, saying she didn't know who'd done it. I wasn't too happy that this would get to Steve's ears, but Robyn was sure it would because Gary Talbot's kid sister was in the same set as her for maths.

On Wednesday we were simply going to get close to each other in the usual scrum coming out of midweek assembly. She was going to scream out and double up as if 'someone' had stuck their elbow in her ribs. Steve and his mates would hear it because the first-years were always sent out first through the back of the hall, where the fourth-years sat. She was going to have to judge it right, though, so that none of the teachers would drag her off to sick bay and find out there was no bruise.

By Thursday we thought we might have to consider sacrificing her school bag or something; but we'd decide for certain later, in case we had any better ideas.

For Friday we were just about stuck. Either we'd have to try varying one of the other tricks, or just think up a kick or tread-on on the spur of the moment.

I'll always remember one thing Laura said that Sunday when we'd got as far as we could with our list for the week.

'You try and make believe that there's no such thing as magic, you two. But look at us here, all three of us, enjoying planning bits of disgusting, violent behaviour –'

'Only pretend,' I said.

'What's the difference? We're all enjoying it, that's what's the trouble. And you wouldn't usually spend your weekends happily planning hitting and stealing and damaging and hurting, would you? But we just have, and yet you seem to think there's no such thing as having an evil spell cast on you.'

I could see what she meant in a way, but I thought she was going too far. We were only trying to find answers to a problem, and that happened to be the problem. If we enjoyed it, that was simply because it was better to make fun of what you could than be all miserable about everything.

One thing I did do that Sunday was to turn and sneak back to the Ziggurat again after I'd made sure they'd gone. This time I didn't hesitate at all, but went straight in, up through the darkness, then slowly, steadily round and round and up to the very top. I didn't even

116

hesitate when I found myself on the flat bit leading to the open doorway, but took the three steps forward till I was under the arch itself.

Here I did stop, but I didn't feel that it was because I was scared to go on. I'm not frightened of heights normally; I'm a good climber, I've got good balance, and there was very little wind this time. It would have been very easy indeed to step out there – perhaps even to go shuffling sideways right round the top with my face towards the turret.

It was just that three questions came into my mind at that moment.

The first was Laura's voice in my ear: 'What *would* happen to your dad if something happened to you?'

The second was a quite sensible voice of my own: '*Why?* Why bother, when there's no one to see and no one to tell?'

The third was also one of my own, and not one I liked, but it was the one that kept nagging and insisting strongest of all: 'How safe *is* that platform, exactly?'

In spite of wanting to conquer that last voice, I didn't stop to try and puzzle out answers. I simply turned and went back down the Ziggurat as steadily as I'd come up. When I got outside at the bottom I looked up to the platform way above. I remember saying to myself, 'Good. I did that. I turned round and came down,' as if that was what I'd meant to do all along, and I remember how much it surprised me that I should feel so OK about it.

The next day disaster struck. I told Steve at break that I was going to get Robyn that evening. I said she'd been away all weekend, and that was why I hadn't been able to hassle her at all then. I told him to be there at the front gate, as he often was anyway, and he'd see something.

What he saw was a mixture of bad luck and bad handling. It started well enough, though, with Robyn, and me just behind her, managing to join on to a big bunch of people going out of the gate. Then out of the corner of my eye I saw Martin Dwyer was right behind *me*.

I knew it was impossible to go ahead with faking Robyn's fall when he was that close, but the trouble was that I panicked. I hissed out 'Robyn!' as loud as I dared and tapped her on the back, meaning to tell her to abort the plan. But because we hadn't planned it well enough, and certainly hadn't allowed for any signal of that kind, she thought I was giving her the signal to do her fall.

Even then things might have been OK if she hadn't done it so badly. But she's not a football player and not used to falling, so the movement she actually performed was more like a kind of sudden 'Gosh, I'm tired!' sit-down. I mean, if you're tripped from behind you go forwards not backwards, and you don't normally have time to put your hands down on the ground first, to break your fall.

Add to that the fact that the people in front of us had parted, so that Steve and Gary – who were both leaning against the wall looking straight at us – had a ringside view of what was happening.

Of course when Robyn sat down I nearly fell over her. I thought quickly enough to try and rescue the situation by giving her a good kick, but I messed that up too, trying not to hurt her. My toe didn't even connect with her backside, and therefore she didn't know to jerk and give a yell as if it had. She just sat there, and not knowing what else to do I sidestepped and went on past her.

'Jake lad! Come here a minute.'

You know how it is when you get caught. You hope against hope that there's been a mistake – that somehow the thing you did wrong hasn't been spotted, or hasn't been seen to be as bad as it actually was. And you know too what a stupid hope that always turns out to be.

Well, that was the way it was this time too. I obediently went over to Steve with that half-hope alive inside me, and it died the moment I saw the expression on his face.

He wasn't angry – yet – but then he had no need to be, seeing how scared I was. He had a sour, disgusted look that I suppose you would have if you'd realized all at once that someone had been both tricking and betraying you for quite a while.

'So you said I'd see something, Jake lad, and I did.' He made the 'Jake lad' sound like swearing.

Martin came up now. He'd obviously twigged the whole thing too, because he asked, 'D'you want me to bring the girl over as well?'

'Naw,' Steve said, as if he was too tired and disgusted to care. 'Plenty of time for her later.'

'I told you not to trust 'im,' said Gary. He was staring at me with so much hate that I knew it was only the fact that some teachers were passing through the gate that saved me from being done there and then.

'Then you were right, weren't you?' Steve said it nastily. It was clear that he couldn't stand being seen to have made a stupid decision.

Perhaps it was partly seeing him caught a bit off guard like that, though mainly it was the feeling that I'd got absolutely nothing to lose now. Anyway, something snapped, and to my surprise I began to feel a huge anger welling up inside me. What the hell was I doing there, trembling in front of this gang of thugs?

There wasn't anything I could do but I just had to do something before *their* anger and threats started. A monstrous, reckless lie sprang into my mind.

'Anyway, Steve Mallinson,' I said. 'You're finished.'

They certainly looked startled, all three of them.

'Yeah,' I went on, spitting the words at him, 'd'you suppose me and Robyn are the only ones against you? There's plenty of us just waiting to get you and your pals.'

Then, in spite of all I was feeling, I had the sense to turn and walk away from them before I could mess it up by trying to say too much. I crossed the road and got on the bus. What was more, I went and sat on the side facing them, staring out at them with a sort of superior smile. They didn't notice me to begin with because they were arguing furiously among themselves. Gary was pointing vaguely in the direction of the bus and for a second I was terrified they were going to get on it too. We might be all right on the bus but there'd be no protection at all once we got to Pikestone.

As the bus started up, they saw me looking. Steve gave me a violent V sign and mouthed a swearword. Gary held up his fist, clenched. Martin just tried giving the same sort of smile I was giving them. I sat staring at them till they were out of sight. Big boys!

And then, of course, I had to move seats and tell Robyn and Laura what I'd done so that we could begin together to count the cost.

Robyn : No Help from Laura!

I was still shaking from everything that had happened by the school gate, then creeping on to the bus and watching Jake in front of them. Now that Jake had finished telling us what had happened – what he'd said to Steve – I felt even worse, if that was possible. Even so, I was absolutely certain at once what had to be done.

'Right, I'm going to get a meeting of everybody for tomorrow lunchtime,' I said. 'We're blooming well going to *have* the plenty of people that Jake told Steve we had. Then he'll see. And you two aren't going to stop me this time.'

'Ro-byn.' Laura was putting on the tired grown-up sort of voice she used sometimes to pour cold water on my ideas. 'Just think, will you? You're going to get loads of people together, right? What are you going to say to them to get them there?'

'I shall tell them what's happened to me and Jake, and I'll tell them we've had enough of it, and it's about time we all stood up to him.'

'And they'll come, will they?'

'I should think they would.'

'They'll come to a place where Steve and his gang can see them?'

'Yes, but there'll be lots, so he won't dare try anything.'

'So you can count on everyone turning up?'

'Well, a few might not.'

'But when they hear how horribly you and Jake are going to be beaten up for going against Steve, the others will all rush to show they're going against Steve, won't they?'

'Well, they . . .' It was no good, though. She was making fun of me and she was right, of course, and I almost hated her for being right. It wasn't the same for her, she wasn't in direct danger. But I wasn't going to give up what *I* knew ought to be done.

'All right then,' I said. 'It's time to start getting help from parents and teachers. We should have done it before, and we've got absolutely nothing to lose now.'

'I think we've been here before,' Jake said. 'I don't care what happens, I'm not involving my dad.'

'Nor me,' said Laura.

For myself, I knew it had got to the stage now where, in spite of everything against it, I was prepared to get my parents' help, and I would have said so if Jake hadn't added, 'Anyway, we *have* got something to lose.'

'What?'

'Two things, really. One is just trying to win this fight ourselves –'

'What's the use of trying to do that if we can't?' I said.

'And the other's just what our mates are going to think of us if we get parents and teachers messing about with something they seem to be all right with.'

'You mean you'd rather risk getting beaten up – no, actually *get* beaten up, because that's what's going to happen – than risk people not liking you?'

'Yes,' said Jake.

He sounded as certain as I wasn't. But anyway, having had my ideas squashed, I hoped at least that they were going to come up with something themselves. I

122

still felt sure that there must be some way of getting more people on our side – after all, in the end Steve only had power over them because they let him. And even if Laura was right and that was what most of them liked, there surely had to be quite a few who didn't, and also some who did but thought it was wrong.

By the end of the journey we had as usual got no further. In fact Laura had said very little and just sat there looking bright-eyed, as if she was thinking very hard about something exciting – which didn't help me and Jake much.

It was Jake who brought out the only two positive things that came from any of us. The first was that actually it might take Steve a day or two to make absolutely certain that what Jake had said *wasn't* true. Even if he did question people about their attitudes, he could never be sure that they were telling him the truth. The second was that we might therefore still have just a little time, but that in any case we ought to stick close to each other.

Laura nodded at both of these but then she suddenly asked, 'Have I to stick with you too?'

'Yeah, I should think so.' Jake sounded as if he was puzzled that she'd even asked.

'You realize that if I do, I'm just going to be added to Steve's hit list or whatever.'

'In that case it's up to you, Laura,' I said. 'Obviously three together is a bit better than two –'

'– but not much,' Jake put in.

'– so you do what you think's best.'

'I will,' she said, and left us without another word.

It was a dismal, terrifying evening, that one, churning the same questions over and over in my mind.

They couldn't actually kill me, could they? Could they? No, you got sent to prison for life for doing that. No one was going to risk a lifetime in prison for a girl who wasn't much more than a nuisance.

Yes, but Steve was practically mad sometimes. Everyone said, and I'd seen it for myself almost. And those people he used – if they hadn't cared about getting chucked out of school, why should they care about getting chucked into prison?

If they didn't kill me, what *would* they do? How much would it hurt? If I flopped down on the ground in a faint the moment I got the first blow, would they believe it and walk off, leaving me alone, or would they go on standing round, kicking at me, like they do in films? And if they did that, mightn't they kill me by accident? That did happen sometimes, I felt sure.

And all these violent scenes where I was the centre were happening in such a shadowy place, with such shadowy figures, apart from me. Where *would* they get me, and who would get me, and would Jake be there being got at the same time?

In between these thoughts I kept looking at my mum and wondering if I ought to, or dared, tell her the danger I was in. She was sitting there in front of the TV, so calm and contented that I couldn't even begin to imagine her getting herself into school and actually stirring others up to do something urgent. What was more, it seemed she'd got a hospital appointment next day over in Marbury, anyway – only a check-up, but she'd have to cancel it completely if I wanted her to go into Ashleigh.

When I looked over at Dad, also in front of the telly but nodding off, it all seemed hopeless getting either of them involved. I'd be certain to end up being patted on the head and told not to worry.

Even worse was the fact that Laura had behaved very oddly when we parted, almost as if she didn't want to have anything more to do with our problems – so oddly that I felt certain it would be useless spending the evening round at her house or on the phone, moaning to her as I would normally have done.

In fact, I did ring her up when I couldn't stand it any longer. I said, 'Laura, I'm so miserable with fright. What shall I do?'

She said, 'Don't worry.'

'Don't worry!'

'No, I think it's going to be all right.'

'What d'you mean, you "think"?'

'I mean I've got an idea.'

'Well, tell me what it is. Please, Laura. I'm going mad here.'

'No, it wouldn't do you any good if I did.'

'But why not?'

'Because you don't believe in the same things as I do.'

'Is it something to do with your magic?'

'I'm not telling you. It wouldn't do any good.'

'Your magic won't do any good.'

'It won't if you don't think it will.'

'Please, Laura, can't you do something?'

'I *am* doing something.'

'But something real.'

'I am doing something real.'

'But really real.'

And so on. In the end she got both angry and bored and hung up on me. I eventually went to bed and had one of those horrible, nightmarish nights where you don't actually have bad dreams you wake up screaming

125

from, but every time you do wake up you feel it's been from a bad dream.

The next morning at school felt nightmarish too. It was a grey day, I remember, and nothing happened all morning. I did notice, though, that the moment the bus arrived Laura dived off into school as if she wanted to keep well away from me and Jake. Martin Dwyer went past me twice in the corridor and Gary Talbot in the yard at break. Neither of them gave any sign that they'd even seen me. I spoke to Jake during the break too, and he reported much the same – nothing at all. We looked around for Laura but didn't see her.

She was there at the beginning of the dinner hour, though. She came pelting past me, even more bright-eyed than ever, panting out in a whisper, 'Follow me.'

I waited a second or two, then followed the direction she'd gone in, round the corner of the science block. It's out of sight of the main playground there, and usually pretty quiet. When I came up to where she was waiting for me, she said at once, 'Where's Jake?'

'I don't think his class has come out yet.'

'OK. I'll stand out here so I can see when he does, and you be out of sight round the corner so no one can see it's you I'm talking to. I've got to catch him before anyone else does.'

'But why –'

She interrupted me very excitedly, 'I've done it, Robyn. I've done it!'

'What have you done?'

'I've fixed Steve. I've made him accept a challenge.'

'A challenge? What sort of challenge? What are you going to do?'

'Not me, stupid. Jake.'

126

'Jake? He never said anything about it at break.'

'He doesn't know yet.'

'He doesn't know?' It was all too confusing for me. 'Laura, please tell me what's going on.'

'I've made Steve accept a challenge from Jake, that's what.'

'But to do what?'

'The Ziggurat, of course.'

'What with the Ziggurat?'

'I don't know. Anything they want. On the top.'

I'd never seen her so excited. 'Laura,' I said, 'just calm down a bit and tell me exactly what you said to Steve.'

'Well, I had to do it quickly, before he had time to discover what Jake told him last night wasn't true. So I went and found him in break. I've never been in that office of his before. It's awful, isn't it?'

'Never mind the office. What did you say?'

'I pretended to be a toad – you know – said I'd come to tell him that a lot of the first-years were getting together against him, but I wasn't one of them. Then I said Jake had been boasting, and that was how he'd got so many of them with him.'

'Boasting! Jake hasn't –'

'No, it's a story! I told him that Jake's been going around saying that Steve's really a coward, and that's why he needs these tough people round him all the time, to protect him. You should have seen Gary Talbot's face – he hadn't a clue whether to look really pleased or very angry.'

'What about the challenge?'

'So I said that Jake says he might not be stronger than Steve, but he's braver, and he's ready to show it any

127

time on the Ziggurat – only I called it the Obelisk so he'd know where I meant.'

'And Steve accepted?'

'No, not straight away. I had to be very clever, because of course Martin Dwyer and Gary Talbot started saying about why should Steve bother with a little jerk like that, and why couldn't they just do him over? And then I said that that was exactly what Jake had told everyone would happen because Steve was such a coward really. Then Steve just said very quietly, "She's right, but that Jake jerk is wrong. I'll go two better than him on anything he wants to try, and we'll do it today."'

'Today! And Jake doesn't even know yet. Is he sure he can do better than Steve? Has he told you he can? And why on the Ziggurat? It's so dangerous. Laura, what *have* you done?'

I was so shocked that for a few moments I forgot the danger I was still in. But I didn't have time to say any more, because she suddenly pointed and said, 'There's Jake, just coming out!' She went to fetch him, saying over her shoulder, 'You're not to say anything at all till I've told him.'

She needn't have worried. Telling someone they've been volunteered for a seriously dangerous job they'd never even thought of is not something I'd actually rush to do myself.

Laura :
Losing Jake

Among many feelings Robyn doesn't understand is what it's like to *know* things. There she was, worried deeply about what I'd done, what Jake would say, why the Ziggurat, and so on. But I *knew*. I knew Jake would take the challenge and I knew the Ziggurat was our only hope because it was where the power lay – the only power strong enough to defeat Steve Mallinson.

All the same, when Jake came up to us it wasn't so easy to begin explaining what I'd done. So what I did was to say quite firmly, 'Look, Jake, I've done something about you that maybe you'll think at first I shouldn't have done. But if you'll just listen till I've told you it all, you'll understand.'

He nodded, and I went ahead.

This time, because I wasn't so excited, I managed to tell it a bit more clearly than I had to Robyn, and he didn't keep interrupting like she had. In fact he listened in complete silence, the way he often does, until I got to Steve's 'today'.

Then he just said very calmly, 'So I've hardly any time to practise – well, maybe that's not such a bad thing. Yeah, OK. It's got to be soon because the longer we leave it, the more chance he'll have of finding out nobody's actually on our side.'

'That's why I did it like that,' I said.

'Then tell him I'll see him as soon as he can get there.

129

I'll go straight from the bus stop.'

Robyn had been bursting to speak and now she felt she could at last. Eyes wide with amazement, she asked him, 'Do you mean you're going to do it, then?'

'Why not?' said Jake. 'It's better than getting beaten up. It could save you from getting beaten up too, if I can do better than him.'

'But you could get killed.'

'No,' said Jake, as if it was a simple fact. 'I'm not going to get killed. And if there's an accident and I do, then I do. After all, our old bus might turn over into a ditch any day.'

'Yes, but this is dangerous. Buses aren't usually. Why aren't you furious with Laura for letting you in for it? I am.'

They both turned to look at me. Robyn did indeed have a furious expression on her face, but Jake didn't.

'No, I think it may be a good idea,' was all he said.

'Well, I don't. I think it's absolutely stupid! I'm having nothing at all to do with it.' She started to walk away from us.

'But we need your help, Robyn,' I pleaded after her. 'We've got to get the others there to see it – as many as possible. It's your chance to get them together. You're always saying you want to.'

'Not for a circus act!' She turned as she snapped at me. 'And if I do, it'll be to get them to stop those two idiots killing themselves.'

To my bewilderment Jake suddenly began to go too, in the opposite direction from Robyn, shouting, 'Tell Steve five o'clock at the Obelisk, then.'

I stood there alone, not knowing which one to run after. Robyn was halfway along the side of the science building, but Jake – almost into the playground – now stopped and turned back towards me. He put his finger to his lips, and I waited, puzzled. I looked for Robyn again, but she'd disappeared round the end of the block. Suddenly I understood. I nodded to Jake. In a moment he was with me again.

'I just wanted to be sure she wouldn't mess things up,' he said. 'Tell Steve a quarter to five. He can get there on his bike almost as quickly as the bus, but it should leave me a few minutes to try out what I can do alone first. Then him and me can get up the Obelisk before Robyn's lot arrives – if she can get anyone to come.'

'The Ziggurat. "Obelisk" is just for Steve, isn't it?' I had to know. I could feel some dark threat looming. Now was the one time that Jake absolutely had to understand and feel and take the power of the Ziggurat.

'Actually I looked it up in the encyclopedia in library period this morning,' he said in his matter-of-fact voice, 'and there's no way it's a ziggurat. Ziggurats were nearer to pyramids, great gigantic things – there was a picture of one – sort of like huge boxes getting smaller and smaller piled on top of each other. And it said you couldn't ever go inside them at all. But that tower thing isn't an obelisk either. I looked that up too, and they're thin and pointy. Really it's just a sort of tower, that's all it is.'

I felt as if a huge cloud, black and cold, had suddenly dropped from the heavy grey sky, covering us both. A small voice inside me was insisting '*It* is *the Ziggurat. It* is *the Ziggurat*' – but it was too small for me to make it heard.

He must have seen how dumb and miserable I was feeling, because he said kindly, 'It's all right. We can go on calling it the Ziggurat if you like.'

131

I went on staring at him, trying not to let him see the blind panic growing inside me. I'd been wrong all this time, and he *didn't* understand – just like Robyn. And if he didn't understand, the Ziggurat mightn't work well for him, and he could be in terrible danger.

There didn't seem to be any chance of explaining. All I could come out with in the end was, 'Perhaps you'd better not do that challenge with Steve.'

He looked a bit surprised but not as much as I might have expected. 'Oh, I'm gonna do it, all right,' he said. 'I don't care what Robyn says.'

He thought I was panicking because of Robyn! It only showed even more strongly how little he understood.

'Are you gonna tell Steve, then, or have I got to?' he was asking. 'It'd be much better if you did.'

'I'll tell him,' I said, but all my enthusiasm, all my feeling of power, had gone. To Jake, it was nothing more than a schoolkid's dare. Maybe I could do something to rescue it, but I wouldn't know whether, or what, till I got to the Ziggurat.

I went off to Steve's office as if I was going to a funeral, trying desperately not to start being afraid that I could be.

Jake : Losing Myself

I didn't see Robyn to speak to that afternoon. I did
catch sight of her several times, though, busy talking
and talking to different lots of our year. She was
obviously working like mad to carry out her threat of
getting people to stop me and Steve doing anything on
the Obelisk. I noticed that as the afternoon went on, the
others started looking at me strangely, but no one said
anything till Rob Bartlett, Kevin Thomas and Stuart
Jones came up to me just before last lesson.

'You aren't really going to try anything against Steve
Mallinson, are you?' Rob asked.

'Looks as if I've got to now,' I said. I didn't want to
explain exactly why I had no choice, because that would
mean saying about having done things for Steve in the
past.

'But he'll walk all over you,' Kevin said.

'If he does, he does. Someone's got to try and stop
him bossing us all about and getting money off us,
though.'

It was only when I saw Stuart gazing at me as if I was
some kind of hero that I realized what I'd said was a lie.
I was going against Steve only because things had
happened in that muddled way and not because I
wanted to Save the School.

'Well, you're either dead brave or dead stupid – or
plain dead, most likely,' he said. 'Do you know Robyn

Somers is trying to get us all to go up there and stop you?'

'I'm going,' said Kevin. 'I know my mum'll let me if I say there's a whole gang of us going.'

'Suppose she tells one of the teachers,' said Rob. 'They'd soon stop it.'

'No,' said Stuart. 'I don't see how they could, outside school. I mean, it's not as if there's anything special about it being at the Obelisk. If you and Steve Mallinson wanted to dare each other chucking yourselves off your own roofs, no one could stop you. Anyway, I'm coming too.'

'To stop me or to watch?' I asked.

Stuart smiled. 'D'you really think I'd bike all that long way just to protect little darling Jakey diddums? No, I want to see you and Steve Mallinson hurtling to the ground together, locked in a deadly embrace.'

'Thanks a billion,' I said, giving a little laugh. It wasn't a very convincing laugh because I wasn't absolutely certain he didn't mean it, but it had given me a possible answer to a worry that had been growing at the back of my mind.

'Listen,' I said. 'What time did Robyn tell you to be there?'

'Five o'clock. Why?'

'Could you come on ahead – get there earlier?'

'I expect we could,' said Kevin. 'I could phone home 'stead of going back there, because I've got my bike here.'

'Please will you?' I asked. 'It could be important.'

They looked at each other to shrug, then nod.

'OK. Suits us.'

Stuart added, 'Don't worry. We'll be there.'

I really felt he meant it and the worry quietened down

a little. It had grown from a sudden picture in my mind – myself at the top of the Obelisk with only Steve (and probably his mates) around, and no witnesses anywhere except maybe Laura.

Robyn wasn't on the bus home and Laura was miserably quiet again – I still couldn't understand exactly why – which did nothing to help calm my quaking guts. I said I supposed Robyn was going to borrow a bike and come on out to the Obelisk with the others, to which Laura only said, 'Yes, perhaps,' then fell silent again.

I felt angry with her. She'd got me into this position and now when I needed her she was giving me no help at all.

Because Laura was being like that, I thought it would probably be worse walking up to the Obelisk with her than going alone, so when the bus finally stopped in the village and we got out, I mumbled something about wanting to have as much time as I could before Steve arrived, and jogged on up ahead.

I'd only done the path up from the village once before. It's about a mile, I should think, and like a lot of the paths on that side of the Pikestone estate, it mostly winds between rhododendron bushes, with occasional clearings of young birch trees and patches where brambles and nettles have taken over, and various turnings-off and forks.

Everything to do with this had happened so quickly that I hadn't had time to do much more than feel nervous, but now as I jogged steadily on up I was planning hard. Steve would certainly know the Obelisk – there was scarcely a person in Ashleigh who didn't – but there was a good chance that he hadn't been up to the top of it for some while. If I could get there a decent amount of time before him – it was still only twenty past four – I could maybe work out something that looked really dangerous but wasn't. Would I dare do anything blindfold, for example, if I got up there and really paced it out exactly so that I'd know without seeing?

I pushed down the thought that I hadn't even been out on the platform yet. There was absolutely no wind today, even though the sky was so grey and heavy that it looked as if it might rain any moment. As for that last time – there'd been no point in trying out anything, though I wished now that I had.

Maybe there were other things I could do, like standing on one leg – I've got good balance – or hopping round the top . . .

The jogging had been seeming a lot easier for some time now. I'd vaguely put it down to getting my second wind, but suddenly the truth broke in on me. I was going downhill. Even as I faltered and stopped I saw a bright green field through the branches ahead. I was on the wrong path. I'd taken a wrong turning somewhere back there.

Just for one moment before I started to panic, I was almost taken over by wanting desperately to go jogging on out into that open green field, forget it all, leave the whole thing behind me.

It wasn't real, though. What was real was the frantic knowledge that I'd now got to find my way back – and uphill too – to the proper path, or else try a short cut directly up through the bushes on my right. As far as I could remember, the last fork had been quite a way back. It was half-past four. If I could get up there in ten minutes or less, I might still have time to try out something before anyone else arrived. Going direct was the only chance.

I was an estate warden's son and I should have known better. In rough country those short cuts always look possible at first, then you find yourself in one mess after another. And the further you go, the more of the messes you've already struggled through you know you'll have to struggle back through if you want to change your mind and return to the nice safe path.

It's just a nightmare blur now, those twenty minutes of panicky stumbling in clawing brambles, eye-poking twigs, thickets of nettles and fallen branches so dense they had to be skirted round. I remember the ruins of a sandstone wall suddenly poking out of the under-growth, and at one point I came face up against a little cliff of about three metres that had to be scrambled up.

The only good thing was that I didn't once lose my sense of direction. After a while, I began to get glimpses of the top of the Obelisk, though that didn't mean I could always go directly towards it. Eventually I staggered out of the bushes into the edge of the clearing and it said ten to five on my watch. There were two separate groups there, waiting: near the base of the Obelisk – Steve, Martin, Gary and Mike; further out in the clearing – Stuart, Rob and Kevin, and Laura with them.

The Wizardry of Steve

I didn't know what to hope as I walked slowly up towards the Ziggurat. That Jake would back down? That Steve would never arrive? That Robyn would arrive early with enough of our year wanting to stop it all? But if I hoped that, why hadn't I gone straight away and told her the trick Jake had played about the time?

In fact I knew nothing except the danger Jake was in. Perhaps if I show you what I wrote in my thoughtbook the evening before, when I decided to use him to challenge Steve Mallinson's wizardry, you'll see better what the matter was:

The Ziggurat was built by the Norman knight Sir Pierre de Brochet in the year 1190 but it was not then called the Ziggurat. Sir Pierre had agreed to accompany King Richard Coeur de Lion on the Third Crusade to Jerusalem, but before he left he wanted to complete this tower, which he said was to display to the whole neighbourhood his rightful power over it. He said that only those with rightful power over the lands they could see from the top could go up it, and he left his brother, Ferdinand de Brochet, in charge of his lands in his absence, which was to last four years.

Ferdinand de Brochet, however, was an evil man who plotted his brother's downfall while he was away, so that he could seize his lands for good. He also hoped to marry Sir Pierre's beautiful wife Leonora if only he could get his brother out of the way. He was hated by Leonora as well as all Sir Pierre's people, for he used them most cruelly.

When news of the Crusaders' return to England spread through the country, Ferdinand spent more and more time at the top of the tower, watching for signs of his brother's approach. While he was up there he also chipped away at some of the stones on one corner of the platform so as to loosen them and make them unsafe.

Sir Pierre finally arrived back, and the first thing Ferdinand did was to take him up to the top of the tower. He said he wanted to show Sir Pierre what good order he'd kept his lands in. Ferdinand got Sir Pierre out on to the platform and told him he ought particularly to look at his castle (which there was then) from there. This was of course from the corner where the stones had been loosened.

But Sir Pierre turned to Ferdinand and said, 'Nay, good brother. Thou has served me well and I must tell thee that my spirit yearns to return at once to the Holy Land. Therefore I do hereby yield into your good care all my lands and my castle too, to hold and keep for always.'

Ferdinand was so shocked and excited by this sudden stroke of good fortune that he forgot everything else, stepping forward eagerly to gaze at the pride of his newly gained possessions – his castle.

The loosened stones gave way beneath his feet, and he fell to his death.

Sir Pierre at once understood what had happened and why. He had learned much about magic on his travels in the lands of the Saracens, and he now put a curse on the tower and secretly called it the Ziggurat, which was a magical kind of tower he had also learned about out there. This curse was that any person who went up the Ziggurat to seek power for himself should meet his downfall there.

I've no idea if that story's true or not. It suddenly came to me when I was trying and trying to think of some way of saving Robyn and Jake from Steve Mallinson, and once it had come I wrote it down and it seemed to give an answer. Jake knew the Ziggurat, I thought at the time, but Steve didn't. Therefore Sir Pierre's curse could only work for Jake and against Steve.

But now that Jake had denied the magic, what could happen? It wasn't the Ziggurat any more to him because he said that a ziggurat was nothing more than a pile of cardboard boxes. That meant he could be as much seeking power for himself as Steve was!

I heard voices behind me and looked round. Three boys I knew from our year, one of them trying to ride his bike up the steep slope, the other two pushing theirs. Perhaps Robyn was going to arrive in time, after all.

'Have you seen Jake? Is he up there?' one of them called to me.

'He should be,' I shouted back. 'He went on ahead. Where's Robyn?'

'Not coming yet. We've come early.'

'Yeah, we didn't half belt here.'

I let them catch up with me, but we didn't say anything else till we came into the clearing and saw no Jake.

'He's probably gone up the Zi— the Obelisk – to practise,' I said.

'Yeah!'

The three of them raced on ahead now. Stuart Jones went straight inside the Ziggurat, calling. It looked as if he wasn't getting any answer, because next moment he'd disappeared up the stairs.

'I don't like it up there,' said Kevin Thomas.

'Nor me neither,' said the third one, whose name I'd forgotten. 'I'm not going in.'

I wasn't either. It was the very last thing I wanted to do just then. I had to be outside where I could think clearly.

140

We heard footsteps coming down quite soon and Stuart reappeared.

'He's not up there. I went right in sight of the top and – hey-up! Here they come.'

We turned in the same direction. It was Steve with his usual three hangers-on, all wheeling bikes across the clearing towards us. Steve looked definitely irritated at finding us already there.

'And where's the little Jake jerk, then?' he asked unpleasantly as soon as he was within talking distance. 'I hope he's not gonna waste my time. I thought he'd be up there practising his pants off.'

'More like gone to find a bog with his pants off,' said Martin Dwyer.

'Or three bogs,' Gary Talbot added pointlessly.

Mike Telford added something even ruder and they all sniggered a bit except for Steve.

'Where is he, then?' This time it was me he was asking.

'I don't know. He came on ahead, but he wasn't here when we got here.'

'Mm,' Steve said thoughtfully. 'You know, if he doesn't come you could well be in trouble too. Anyway, since he isn't here, *I'm* gonna have a practice. Any objections?'

It wasn't likely that there would be, but we all dutifully shook our heads. Steve propped his bike up against the wall of the base, then slowly walked along to the entrance and went inside. We listened to his footsteps growing gradually fainter.

The three hangers-on and the three boys began to talk quietly in their separate groups. I turned and walked a little way off so that I'd be able to see Steve when he appeared at the top. You can't, of course, see anything on the platform if you're too close to the bottom of the Ziggurat.

It wasn't long before I saw him framed in the doorway at the top; a tiny figure that reminded me of something – I couldn't place what – something mechanical. The figure hesitated and craned forward with its arms outstretched, obviously holding on to the sides of the doorway arch. So Steve Mallinson wasn't without fear.

But then the figure moved forward, then sideways, and began to edge round the turret, slowly, arms still out, feeling his way round. I couldn't even tell if he had his face or his back to the wall of the turret. He was moving in the direction of the broken-off corner first. For a few seconds when he was right by it, I saw his side view silhouetted against the sky – it was his back that was against the wall – then he gradually edged further round, out of sight.

I waited. There was no point in running to see him the other side. He'd appear soon – and sure enough he did, still edging slowly, but perhaps not quite as slowly. He was getting more confident.

I expected him to go in at the doorway when he got back to it, but then he started round again, this time walking normally, not with his back to the wall. As he reached the broken corner and I could see him against the sky, I noticed he had one hand on the wall to steady himself.

Next time he reappeared, then passed the doorway, the broken corner, he had no hand against the wall. As far as I could tell at that distance, he was almost strolling, hands in pockets maybe.

Next time he began to move more quickly. He was trotting now! He went round five times like that at a steady pace, then suddenly turned in at the doorway, presumably on his way down.

'Jake'll never do that – not in a year of blue moons. And even if he does, Steve Mallinson'll find something better to do.'

It was Stuart Jones with the other two. I'd been concentrating so hard on Steve, I hadn't noticed them come up beside me. They were all nodding in agreement.

'I expect he'll have a go, though,' Kevin Thomas said – loyally, but without a lot of hope in his voice.

I still didn't know what to say or think. Steve had reappeared at the bottom, where his mates were waiting. I could see him pointing up, telling them what he'd done. Their excited voices and harsh laughter carried to us across the still clearing.

Then there was a rustling of leaves, a crackling of twigs, and a figure emerged out of the bushes not far from us. It was Jake at last.

Jake : Facing Up

I went to my own group first, in spite of the jeers and catcalls from Steve and his mates. I knew they thought I was late because I was scared, but nothing I could say was going to make that lot believe any different anyway.

They weren't looking happy – Laura specially not – as I came up to them.

'I took the wrong path and got lost,' I said.

'Well, you've given Steve Mallinson a great chance to go up there and practise,' said Stuart.

'Yeah, and you've got your work cut out, I'm telling you.'

Laura said nothing, only gazed sadly at me as if I was already a goner. She was a great encouragement!

It was obvious that none of them were going to offer to tell me what Steve had actually done up there – probably because they didn't want to put me off – so I said, 'Right, I'll get it over with, then,' and started over towards the Obelisk, the rest following. I tried hard to walk straight and not show how shaky I was from the combination of nerves and my efforts getting there through all that jungle.

Steve was sitting on top of the base, his legs dangling over the entrance. 'So Jake jerk's finally decided to turn up, has he?' he said loudly. 'Right, then, we're gonna do this by the book. As Jake jerk is the challenger, *and* he's chosen the place too, I'm gonna say what we do.

144

Has anyone got a watch with a stopwatch function?'

Mike Telford and Stuart both said, 'Yeah.'

'Well, that's lucky – one each side. In that case they're gonna time us from down here, and the contest is five laps of the platform, shortest time's the winner. Any objections?'

For a second or two it didn't seem such a bad idea – from down where we were then, anyway – and I felt I might be able to face it. 'Can I have a practice first?' I asked. 'You have.'

Steve leant forward on his perch to glare down at me. 'Look, Jake jerk, you live near here. You chose the place. If I had a practice just now it was only to even things up a bit. No way.'

'All right, then, I don't accept,' I said. 'That wasn't the challenge.'

'I've just said what the challenge is.'

'Well, it isn't now. I don't accept.'

There was a short pause while Steve looked baffled. Then he said nastily, 'What's the matter? Scared, are you?'

'Of course I'm scared trying to do something you've just practised and you know you can do. What you said to Laura was that you'd go two better than me on anything I wanted to try.' I turned. 'Didn't he, Laura?'

She nodded.

'So what are you gonna try, then?' asked Steve. 'I've a right to know, haven't I?'

'I'd tell you if I knew myself, but I won't know till I'm up there.' That was certainly true. There was a glimmer of an idea forming in my mind, but I wasn't sure quite what it was, or if I'd be able to pull it off.

'And what does the winner get?' It was Laura's voice from behind.

Steve was a bit taken aback. He obviously hadn't thought about it, and nor had I.

'OK, then,' he said. 'If the Jake jerk wins whatever he thinks he's gonna do, he gets no more hassle from me or my mates – but he won't.'

'What about Robyn?' came Laura's voice again.

'All right, that creep too, then, as long as she keeps off my back in future.'

'And what about me – and the rest of our year?'

'Aw, what's the difference? OK, I'll lay off the whole of your year.'

'And what if you win?'

'Ah, now you're talking sense. After I've won, Jake and you and anyone else in your year agree to do anything I say with no questions and no complaints. Right?'

'They do that already,' said Martin. 'Why don't you get some money off 'em?'

'Yeah, 50p a head,' said Gary. 'Come in handy, that would.'

It was Stuart who answered that one. 'Jake's no right to promise money from people that aren't here.'

'He can pay it himself, then,' said Steve carelessly. He pushed himself off his perch and dropped to the ground. 'Come on. I'm fed up talking. Let's get up there and do it before I'm bored out of my skull. You first, Jake jerk. Then you can show us your fancy tricks before I go two better. That's what I said, isn't it?'

Everyone nodded agreement and I led the way in and up the stairs. We'd only gone a few steps before I heard footsteps pattering in below and Laura's voice came echoing up.

'Robyn's just arrived! She's got the most gigantic gang of our year with her.'

There wasn't anything to answer, so I didn't and nor did Steve. We just continued on and up into the darkness.

Robyn : Defeat

'Where are they?' I yelled to Laura as soon as I thought she could hear. She was just coming out of the entrance to the Ziggurat. I could see Steve's thugs, and I could see a little group of Jake's friends, but I couldn't see the two people who really mattered.

Laura jerked her thumb back and up to the Ziggurat behind her.

'Oh *no*, Laura! How *could* you let them?'

'How could I stop them?'

'But it's –' I looked at my watch. 'We're only a minute late.' She could have no idea what a brilliant, brilliant piece of organization it had been getting fifty – sixty? – maybe nearly a hundred people on to bikes, parents warned (I hoped) about late arrival back, along the road and up the path to get here all together and only one minute late. And now it seemed it was one minute *too* late. I was nearly crying with vexation and fear.

'We've got to stop them!' I shouted.

What was more, there were discontented mutterings now from behind me. To be honest, I had no idea whether they were caused by us arriving too late or by what I'd just said. The whole afternoon had been a flurry of getting people to agree to come and getting them to tell other people to come. I wasn't certain how many of them had eventually arrived here because they

148

wanted to stop the stupid contest from happening and how many because they wanted to see it happen.

'Why have we got to stop them?' someone shouted from behind me. 'Let 'em get on with it.'

There was a large chorus of 'Yeah!' in support.

In spite of this I yelled out, 'We're going up there to tell them to come down,' sweeping my arm forward as a signal and starting towards the entrance. 'Come on!'

I didn't look round to see, but it wasn't difficult to sense that no one was following me. Still I went on, but as I got near to the entrance Steve's three thugs slowly moved across it, blocking my way.

'Let me past!' I screamed at them.

'You and whose army?' said Gary Talbot.

'It'll be murder! You'll end up in gaol for life!'

'Suicide maybe,' Martin Dwyer sneered, 'but no one's going to have to kill your little darling boy. He'll do that for himself.'

There came a sudden 'Ooh!' of excitement from the crowd out in the clearing. I looked round. Every face was turned up towards the top of the Ziggurat. The three thugs ran out to see, leaving the way clear.

'Get on up there if you want,' Gary shouted over his shoulder as he ran. 'But you're too bloody late.'

I was, I knew it. Ashamed and desperate, I ran back to join the others.

When I turned it was to see someone framed in the doorway at the top, holding on to the sides of the arch.

'It's Jake,' said Laura, just beside me. 'Steve's not wearing a sweater.'

'Get on with it!' someone yelled out, but I knew they'd be able to hear almost nothing up there.

As if in answer the figure dropped its arms. There

149

was utter silence in the clearing. Then the figure turned and disappeared inside.

'And is that it?' (Martin Dwyer's jeering voice from somewhere near.)

'I could do *that*,' a disgusted voice came from the crowd.

'Yeah, what's he playing at?'

'Steve'll slaughter him.'

The hush fell again as another figure appeared in the doorway. The white top told us that it was Steve.

The figure moved forward a little.

'Looks just like a cuckoo coming out of a clock,' Laura muttered.

Next moment she suddenly went wild. She dashed out in front of the crowd, dancing absurdly, stabbing a pointing finger upwards, shrieking, 'Look! Look! The cuckoo's come out of the clock! See the cuckoo, everyone!' She twisted round, cupping her hands to her mouth, screaming harshly, 'Cuckoo!' Cuckoo!'

An answering ripple of noise grew quickly till it became a hubbub of jeering, cheering, whoops of laughter, catcalls. Someone let out a piercing cuckoo whistle.

I don't know exactly what sort of noise carried up to the top of the Ziggurat, but it must have sounded like applause, because the figure bowed as though in response, spreading its arms out.

'Cuckoo!' screamed Laura in time with the bow.

'Cuckoo!!' answered the crowd.

The figure bowed again twice, each bow spreading its arms like wings, and the crowd yelling, 'Cuckoo! Cuckoo' in time with it, Laura's voice shrieking in a frenzy above the rest.

Then the figure turned sideways and began a little

jogging run. It passed the broken corner and disappeared behind the turret. The moment it reappeared at the other side, the mad chorus of 'Cuckoo!' went up, and on till the figure disappeared again. Five laps the figure did, and each time the crowd kept on cuckooing and jeering it round till it went out of sight.

At the end of the fifth lap it stopped in front of the doorway, turned to face us, bowed once more – 'Cuckoo!!' – and then it went in.

There followed a tiny uncertain pause till someone shouted out, 'There's Jake now!' At first I looked wildly for him on the platform, but he was down in the entrance. The crowd dropped their bikes where they were and we all surged forward towards the base of the Ziggurat. Jake stayed on the entrance step, waiting, till the crowd had surged up and gathered round. He looked as dazed and defeated as anyone could have expected.

'Bloody useless coward!' The cry brought its usual accompaniment of jeers and catcalls.

'OK – OK –' Jake was trying to make himself heard above the noise.

'Listen to him, you morons!' Laura's screeching voice pierced through the noise, and it quietened a little.

'I just wanna say –' Jake shouted, 'I only wanna say that the challenge was that Steve would go two better on anything I did.'

'You did nothing.'

'Yeah! You chickened out.'

'What I did was when I got out there, I decided it was too dangerous to play games on –'

'Yellow-belly!'

'– and I told Steve Mallinson that if he wanted to

show off what a big shot he was, he could, but if anything happened to me it'd kill my dad and I wasn't going to. I didn't mean to do that, but that's what I did. So let him go two better than that if he ca—'

A sob took the last word away from him. There was an embarrassed silence. Jake put his arm across to cover his eyes, stepped down and stumbled along the base wall to the corner, then out of sight. I wanted to run after him but now Steve appeared in the entrance, hands clenched above his head, a triumphant grin on his face.

'So much for your hero and his old dad,' he shouted. 'Which means –'

'Cuckoo!' This time Laura said it almost sweetly, as if all she needed to do was to give the signal.

And it worked. The chorus of 'Cuckoo!' which burst out at once all around was so deafening and continuous that it might almost have been heard away in Ashleigh. And I was cuckooing with the best.

The expressions coming and going on Steve's face were so extraordinarily quick-changing that the effect was almost pathetic. At first it was a sort of shy smile, as if he thought we were still in some way applauding, then it became bewilderment deepening to suspicion, then annoyance as he tried to make himself heard but couldn't. Finally there was understanding – anger – fury.

From the front, right close to him, I could a bit hear what he was trying to say. It was much what you'd expect – 'I'll get you for this. You'll pay for this' – that sort of thing. I tried yelling back, 'Not all of us, you won't,' but I'm sure he didn't hear me.

He didn't need to, anyway. He knew it was over. He gave murderous look after murderous look as though he wanted to screw up enough courage to launch himself into us with fists flying. He stared wildly around for his thugs to help him, but they also knew there were too many of us, and they'd been down with us when the cuckooing first started. They were already wheeling their bikes away, nearly out of the clearing.

In the end Steve gave up. With a final snarl he stepped down and shambled round to where his bike was propped against the base. I noticed how careful he was not to jostle anyone, twisting his body awkwardly sideways in order to avoid contact. I could see he was terrified that if he made one false move the whole crowd might tear him to pieces.

And all this time the cuckooing continued. It went on around him as he fumbled with his bike, it pursued him across the clearing, and he must have heard the final dying whistles and calls even after he'd left our sight.

Laura : So Who Lost?

Robyn thinks that's all there is to tell, but I don't. In fact, the one real quarrel we had over writing it was about this last bit. It was only when I said we'd have to take a vote on it that Robyn caved in. She knew Jake would be bound to side with me because he could never be happy about finishing with that last picture of him slinking away out of sight behind the Ziggurat.

Yet in a way that was exactly the picture of him Robyn wanted to end with. She's still sure she was right all along – that the thing which really defeated Steve was her getting everybody together to show that they were against him. She said it was only chance that it happened to be at the Ziggurat and that Jake happened to be challenging Steve.

'I mean, let's face it,' she said. 'Jake failed, didn't he?'

That wasn't the way lots of others saw it. One of the strangest results was the way that instead of blaming Jake for losing his nerve up on the Ziggurat, they began to talk as if he'd defeated Steve in the way he'd meant to – 'Didn't Jake do great up there?' sort of thing. He became quite a hero for our year, and he's still one of the most popular in it.

Robyn says that just shows what tiny memories some people have, and how they'd rather have a hero to tell them what to think and show them what to do, than think and do for themselves. At the same time, it doesn't exactly prove *her* point, does it?

As for me, I know what really happened, of course. It was the Ziggurat that won after all. The Ziggurat gave us the time, the place, the event, and finally it spoke the right words to me. Its magic is infinitely more powerful than Steve's ever was, and it simply took his magic away from him for daring to think he'd conquered it.

I saw the truth of that the very next day. There he was, walking across the playground with his usual swagger, when a little group of third-years, who'd heard the story but hadn't had the joy of shouting at him, began making cuckoo noises – you know, hiding their faces at first, the way you do with a teacher, so that he couldn't actually see who was doing what, testing him out.

And d'you know, he didn't even begin to try and deal with it. He just looked over towards them and gave them a little sheepish grin then went on past. And they, of course, having lots of old scores to settle, began letting loose openly, with all the whooping and catcalls and cuckooing we'd all been doing the day before.

A lot of that sort of thing went on for more than two weeks after – until we broke up for the summer, in fact – and all Steve ever did was smile nervously. When we came back into the second year, Steve was just another fifth-year working for his GCSEs, and everything we knew and felt about him might just as well have been about someone else.

Yet I lost some of my magic too. You can't call the thing you've always felt to be more truly grand and magical than anything else a cuckoo clock, and still feel it to be grand and magical. None of us went near the Ziggurat for a long time after. We told each other it was too dangerous, and that anyway the Pikestone caves were just as exciting.

The other day, though, something strange happened. Robyn leant over to me on the bus home and whispered, 'Laura, you know Paul Jackson in the fifth year? Well, everyone says he really likes me, and I like him a bit, and I don't know what to do.'

Then, suddenly, I knew what that fourth window of the Ziggurat had been waiting for. Suddenly the feeling of a whole new world of magic came flooding back . . .

Robyn : . . . but that's another story altogether.